Doppelgänger

A Harbour Bay Novel

Camille Taylor

Doppelgänger

Limitless Publishing, LLC
Kailua, HI 96734
www.limitlesspublishing.com

Formatting: Limitless Publishing

ISBN-13: 978-1-68058-681-7
ISBN-10: 1-68058-681-5

Prologue

Hot tears rolled down Angel Bellman's cheek. Her throat was hoarse from screaming, her nails broken. The skin on her fingers had torn open and were bleeding from when she'd clawed at the concrete wall in the darkened room.

The air inside the small space was stagnant and cold as death, which was appropriate, because the room reminded her of a crypt. She was sealed in with no escape. She bit back the sob that rose, and her whole body shook as she slumped against the rough, biting wall and slid to the dirt floor. She'd even tried to dig her way out, but the ground was too hard, almost like clay beneath her fingertips.

Glancing up at the red and greenish-yellow glow from the video camera mounted high in the corner of the room, she knew someone was watching her, enjoying her suffering. The glow was the only source of light. Whoever was watching had no demands of her, making her all the more desperate. She would gladly do anything—and she meant *anything*—to get out of this dark hole, her grave.

She tried to swallow, but her mouth refused to produce saliva. She was so thirsty and as humiliating as it was, she'd even drunk her own pee, yet now her body refused to even produce that temporary relief. Hunger had become a thing of the past—something she barely remembered feeling. With each passing day, she became weaker and closer to death.

How long had she been in this prison? Time had no meaning to her and she had no way to track it. Was anyone even looking for her? Did they know she was missing? Why had she run away from home? Why had she left her mother's trailer? Sure, it was no way to live, but it had been better than being on the streets. At least she'd had a roof over her head and food in her belly. At least she'd been free to come and go as she pleased, even if she wasn't completely safe from her mother's many boyfriends.

Her clothes were torn and dirty and she tried once more for the man to take pity on her. "Please let me go. Please. I won't tell anybody, I promise. Just please let me go." Her voice cracked.

Silence greeted her.

She'd alternated between begging and threatening the man who held her against her will and was once again pleading for her life. What did he want from her? The obvious answer was sex, but he'd not made a single overture towards her. She'd laughed at the idea of a ransom. The man had taken her from the alley she'd been camped out in behind a restaurant. He was stupid if he believed he'd get a dime for her.

The man had made no contact with her since taking her and it was freaking her out. She wrapped her arms around her raised knees and wearily rested her head against her legs. She was so tired but feared closing her eyes, wondering if she would ever open them again.

She startled when a hiss escaped the vents above her head. A smoky cloud descended, filling the room quickly. Her skin became sticky to the touch as whatever it was settled on her. Her throat began closing and she coughed violently as the vapour filled her airways and was sucked deep into her lungs.

Oh God, she was suffocating!

Angel pushed up and stumbled into the corner furthest from the vents as agony tore through her. She hit her head against the wall as she gasped, trying to breathe. Her vision blurred and her legs gave out. She collapsed and her body flailed on the cool, dirt floor.

She cried out as the pain overwhelmed her. Her lungs burned and her organs began to shut down. She was terrified, then she felt nothing at all. No pain, no fear, just numbness. When she was no longer able to hold a coherent thought, she welcomed the darkness.

Chapter 1

As he stared at the body that had been dumped alongside the old highway, Detective Senior Sergeant Dean Matthews swore. Having arrived only moments ago, he looked to his partner, Nicholas Doyle, for confirmation. He didn't need it, though, because his gut had already told him.

It was barely past six in the morning and Nick had been first on the scene before calling in Dean, waking him from a deep sleep in the first few hours of his well-deserved twenty-four-hour hiatus.

A light breeze blew against his face, choking him with the pungent scent of decomposing flesh. Swallowing back the bile, he listened as Nick confirmed his worse fears.

"MO matches—dark haired girl in her late teens or early twenties. Her fingernails are broken and the skin's been shredded."

"Fuck! That's the fifth one so far. I want this guy strung up by his balls."

The sentiment was felt throughout the LAC. Every available detective had been reassigned to help solve the Highway Dumper murders. He'd spent the past ten months trying to find the guy after Dean had been given lead on the case by his former boss, Superintendent Harris, who had retired almost seven months ago. It had been a touchy case. One that had almost been caught in a jurisdiction war when the body of Carolyn Harper had been found by the side of the King George Highway not far from where they now stood. Her remains had been on the border between Harbour Bay and the next town over. Chief Gregory Fallon of the Heavenly Police Force had been reluctant to let the body go and they'd almost been too happy to let him have it.

Over the past few years, the relatively small city of Harbour Bay had seen its fair share of murders. The once booming tourist town was only just beginning to get some of its tourists back. The coastal town of roughly three hundred thousand lay southeast of Sydney, nestled against a sea-green harbour and the small bay for which it was named.

Dean bent down over the body. The skin of the deceased was almost black with dirt and bugs. She appeared to have not bathed in some time. He added that to his mental notebook. Wherever these women were being held, there was little chance of there being running water. The autopsies of the other unfortunate victims showed dehydration as well as starvation.

"How long?"

Nick gave another quick perusal of the deceased before straightening and taking some deep breaths of fresh air probably in an effort to settle his rebelling stomach. Even Dean was feeling a little green. "Ten to twelve days ago."

Shit, already that long? How the hell had no one noticed a dead girl on the side of the highway? It had taken several crows circling above for someone to venture near expecting to see a dead kangaroo and had lost their breakfast when they'd come across the crows' feast.

"That fucker probably already has another victim. How's the evidence coming?"

Looking over at him, Nick shook his head. "Not good. It rained here twice in the past four days. Any evidence has been washed away."

Dean wanted to hit something. This was no ordinary psycho. He had already killed five women, and he wouldn't stop until he was caught.

"That's not good enough. Find me something—anything."

After giving the decedent another look, he stormed back to his car. He didn't need to stay. He'd already seen five replicas of the crime scene to know there was nothing there that would help him. The perpetrator was either extremely good or very fucking lucky. He climbed into his car and sat staring out his window.

"I'm going to find you. No doubt about it," he said to himself.

Chapter 2

After typing the last sentence on her laptop, Megan Bailey hit *control S*, saving her document. She sat back in her favourite chair, a large recliner with thick soft cushions. She was done. Now she just had to print the document and hand it over to her editor. But first she had to buy paper. Between herself and her younger cousin Stacey, they went through paper like it was going out of style, though they both had good reason.

She'd already written three bestsellers. This would be her fourth and she prayed it would be as well received as the last. Stacey was a student and often had to print her essays for class. She'd come to stay with Megan when she'd been accepted at Harbour Bay University. All Megan asked for was silence, which suited them both, as they each had to concentrate. The slightest distraction could prove disastrous.

Hearing the sound of cereal being poured into a bowl, she wandered through the wide arch that separated the family room from the entryway and kitchen of her apartment. Stacey was up, and had been for some time, since she'd already showered and was dressed for school. She smiled at Megan before adding milk to her bowl.

A mirror image of herself, something that had only began to show when Stacey was in her teens. They both favoured their fathers; Liam and Damien Bailey had been twins. Both girls were five-foot-four and both had green eyes, and dark mahogany hair hanging just past their shoulders. The hairstyle hadn't been planned. Stacey got her hair cut prior to moving in with Megan and they'd both had a chuckle over the coincidence.

The only difference between them was a few kilos and the eight years separating their births.

"You've been awake all night, haven't you?" Stacey asked.

The pot calling the kettle black. Stacey had spent more than one night hunched over her computer or text book studying. Despite powering through the night, Megan felt rejuvenated, riding the high she always got when she completed a novel. She nodded. "I'm finished."

Stacey clapped and jumped up and down before granting Megan a giant bear hug and almost blinded her with perfect white teeth as she smiled excitedly.

"Oh, I can't wait to read it. It's so great being an author's cousin, you know. I get to read the bestsellers before they're even printed."

Smiling ruefully, Megan said, "I don't know where you find the time to read my books when you're busy with school."

"I make time, that's how."

Stacey took a mouthful of cereal and chewed before speaking. "Have you told Riley yet?"

Riley was her editor. "No. I'm going to call her later. Oh, I'm also going to the shop today to get more paper. Do you need anything?"

"Nope, nothing I can think of," she replied before shovelling more cereal into her mouth.

Megan stretched, feeling more human as she removed the kinks from her body. "I'm going to have a shower. You have fun at school."

Stacey frowned. "Yeah, sure, it's a blast listening to the monotone voices of my professors."

"Yep, don't miss it at all," Megan said.

"Don't be late home. Pizza night tonight," Stacey added.

It was something they did every week, a way to catch up since they both had hectic schedules. It was a night they allocated to each other. No writing, no studying, no dates—no one but the two of them and a Hawaiian pizza.

Megan nodded. "Don't worry, I won't miss pizza night."

Three hours later, she was sitting in Riley O'Neill's office in the heart of the city. The building that housed B&G was new, having been built a couple of years ago, and was all glass and chrome which suited the corporate look the publishing house went for. It occupied eight of the twelve floors of the building and was one of the largest companies in Harbour Bay.

The floor in the lobby was polished ivory marble, each floor having its own distinct feel and colouring. Level six where Riley worked was a fuchsia with dark paint on the walls, a lighter shade for the seats, a dark stain wood flooring which held thousands of tiny pinpricks from stiletto heels. The ceilings were high, causing any sounds to echo loudly and the entire west side was open to the view from floor to ceiling length windows. The offices were small, except for the offices of the big executives like Riley, and seemed about as personal as a cell.

Riley's office was on the north side and she was lucky enough to have an external wall.

Megan loved Riley. She spoke her mind and was quick to offer constructive criticism, which helped greatly when it came to getting her books on the bestseller lists. She was petite, about five-foot-five in the heels she always wore.

Her red hair was wild, the red ringlets framing her face and pale Irish skin. Along with her wide, deep blue eyes, she was a package no man could walk past without a second long, lingering glance Riley always failed to notice. According to her, she was the only one in the family who truly looked Irish. Her much older brother Declan looked nothing like her except for his eyes; she'd shown Megan a photo of him, a very smoking hot guy with blond hair. There was no denying the resemblance.

Today, Riley was dressed in one of her expensive suits—Chanel or something equally well-known on the catwalk. Megan knew she didn't buy her own clothes and didn't give a stuff about fashion. She made the money and her assistant, Michelle, did the buying since Riley was a high-powered executive who didn't have time to peruse

Myer's new collection. The only accessory Riley cared about were her shoes, and today she was wearing Jimmy Choo size sevens.

Riley looked down at the manuscript in front of her. "I know I'm going to love this, Megan. I'll read it as soon as I can."

Once, she'd believed that to be a brush-off but Riley really meant it. Every night, she went home and read the dozens of manuscripts that budding and hopeful authors sent in weekly to the publishing house. While most of the other agents passed that job to their assistants, this was one thing in Riley's life that Michelle didn't handle.

"So how is everything lately?" Riley asked, referring to the hate mail Megan had gotten a while back. It was addressed to her apartment and not the publishing house where most hate mail went for the agents to inspect for security reasons.

The hate mail wasn't what bothered her. She knew as her popularity rose, so would the public's attention, and not everybody was a fan. No, what bothered her was that whoever had sent the letter had addressed it to Megan Bailey as opposed to Meredith Baker, her pen name. The reason she used a pseudonym was so she could still have some anonymity.

"Fine. Nothing else has come to the house, so I assume they've moved on."

Riley nodded. "Well, you call me right away if you get more, okay? I need to know these things and not several months *after* the fact."

Megan raised her hands in surrender. "Yes, *Mother*."

There was a knock on Riley's door and Michelle entered with a stack of mail.

"Hi, Megan," the bubbly assistant said.

"Hey, Michelle, how's things?"

"Going good. Heard you finished your new book. I can't wait to read it."

"You'll have to get in line. My cousin Stacey said the same thing this morning."

Michelle placed large envelopes on Riley's desk, adding to the clutter. Megan had never seen Riley's desk neat and tidy, and was sure that even Riley had no idea what colour the wood was beneath all the paper.

Riley frowned at the large stack on her desk. "What's all this?"

Michelle rolled her eyes and made quotation marks with her fingers when she spoke. "Mr. Big Shot Johnson refuses to take unsolicited mail anymore. He's sick of every 'Tom Dick and Harry' thinking they can 'write.'"

Riley cast an unamused look at Michelle. "Oh, Jesus, how does he expect to find great writers unless he reads the books they send?"

"I guess he assumes they'll just fall out of the sky and into his lap."

Riley raised an eyebrow, and Megan knew she had a dirty comment in mind, but held her tongue. Megan counted the envelopes on the desk. Ten were waiting to be opened. She felt immensely happy that she was now a published author. Looking at the pitiful novels lying sealed in large envelopes, she was surprised she'd managed to become a professional author. It seemed so hopeless and daunting, her dreams at the hands of someone like 'Mr. Big Shot Johnson' who threw out material without looking. She was thankful Riley had taken the time to read her manuscript without immediately dismissing it. Megan suddenly had a lot more respect and appreciation for Riley.

Chapter 3

The TV blared where Dean sat in the Highway Dumper's Taskforce Command Centre.

"Earlier this morning, the body of a young woman was discovered just outside of Harbour Bay. Police are tight-lipped over the circumstances of her death, however, this is the fifth body found discarded on the side of the King George Highway. The victim is still unidentified at this time, but sources say she has been dead for several days and the LAC still have no leads as to who is committing these horrific murders..."

Dean blocked out the incessant drawl of the reporter who was berating him and his team for being unable to track down the killer. As if he wasn't already blaming himself for the young woman's murder. If at any time over the past few months he'd been able to catch the bastard, numerous lives would've been saved. Unfortunately, tracking a murderer wasn't as easy as TV led people to believe.

He looked up at the long white board that had a permanent place in the command centre—a repurposed conference room just off the bull pen that housed the LAC's Detective Unit. The crime scene photos of the five victims were grotesquely displayed under the snapshots of their smiling faces prior to their deaths. The meagre information they had was neatly written on the board below the pictures. A profile had been made up and the main points were written on the far right hand side of the board—descriptions that weren't at all helpful until they had someone to compare them to.

Dean turned as he heard heavy footfalls approach. Nick made his way towards him, his face stoic.

"Jane Doe is now Angel Bellman," he announced. "Her fingerprints were on file after she was arrested a few years ago for theft. Her residence is listed as the caravan park on Wheeler. Her mother is still there but can't remember the last time she saw her daughter. Apparently, they fought over the mother's latest boyfriend and Angel left."

Dean frowned. Their perp had a type. He took people who wouldn't be easily noticed—runaways, mostly, women he could get his hands on. Which meant he was either extremely charming or he ambushed them.

"What about the boyfriend?"

"A piece of work. He admitted to being fresh with her, but Angel took off before it could go any further. Hasn't seen her since." The look on Nick's face said it all. "As much as I want it to be him just so I can lock the prick up, I'm not convinced. This guy couldn't arrange a fuck in a brothel let alone mastermind several abductions."

Dean rubbed a hand over the back of his neck.

"I canvassed the area where most of the homeless hang out and found a few who recognised her."

Harbour Bay, like any city, had its fair share of homeless, but mostly they were harmless and didn't cause problems.

"I was able to narrow down the timeframe," Nick continued. "Angel and a couple women went clubbing five weeks ago. They 'lucked out' and called it a night. The next day Angel was missing."

So that was how she was making money. An easy way to pick up potential clients and no way for the cops to cry prostitution or soliciting. The idea of the young woman selling her body to stay alive pissed him off. Her mother should've protected her.

Dean rested his hands on the table and stared up at the white board, willing it to give him something to go on—anything. Five women were dead and he was no closer to finding the killer than he was ten months ago.

"Think he was a john?" Nick asked, interrupting his thoughts and self-recriminations.

Dean immediately dismissed the idea. "There's been no indication of sexual assault on the victims. All were discovered fully dressed and their bodies unmarked except for the injuries they inflicted on themselves trying to free themselves of whatever prison he kept them in." He let out a frustrated breath as Nick ran a hand through his dark hair.

"We have to catch this prick. Five victims in ten months that we know of, and the last just a few months before the next. With the way he's escalating, he would've already chosen his next victim by now."

Chapter 4

Stacey walked through the campus grounds, feeling anxious about the exam she would take in a few weeks. She never tested well on demand and knew she would have to work hard to keep her grades up.

She was studying business and hoped to start her own art gallery one day, but she knew she had a long way to go. She had a good head for numbers and she loved art and even took it as an elective, but she didn't have the patience to be artist even though she loved to paint. She was constantly being told she had the talent, but she couldn't seem to follow through when it came to painting.

She'd won many prizes over the years for her art and had once seriously considered going down that path until her mother had vetoed it. She was the one paying the bills, so she wanted to see results. Anyone could put paint on a canvas, was her mother's opinion. It was an entirely different thing to have an accountant's licence or a business diploma.

She loved her mother, but sometimes felt smothered by her. Her father had died ten years ago when she was still a child and her mother had never remarried, making Stacey an only child. She'd received all of her mother's unwanted attention and high expectations, and was constantly in fear of disappointing her. She thought she might collapse one day under the pressure of living up to the image her mother had in mind.

Although Megan didn't know it, she had been offered positions at the likes of Charles Stuart Uni, Charles Darwin, and the Australian National University in Canberra but none had appealed to her.

She wanted to be close to Megan. She'd always looked up to her cousin and had practically been raised with her before Megan's life had taken a turn for the worse and she'd moved away. They were closer than cousins, more like sisters. Did Megan feel the same? She certainly treated Stacey as if she did, and supported her no matter what she wanted to do. After years of her mother dictating what she should do, it was a welcome change.

She remembered the night they'd gotten drunk while celebrating Megan's bestseller status and Stacey had recklessly blurted out her dreams of opening Bailey's Art Gallery. She regretted being so open and feared Megan might tell her mother, who would immediately stop paying for her schooling in retaliation. But she'd been surprised when Megan had encouraged her and promised to be her first customer. Megan further shocked Stacey when she'd told her that if her mother didn't like the reasons she was going to school and refused to pay, she would gladly foot the bill. Stacey had been speechless.

She heard her name being called and came out of her reverie, then turned to see one of her professors running towards her. Stopping, she waited for him to catch up.

"Professor Todd?" she said when he drew close.

He reached into his pocket and pulled out an envelope and handed it to her. "This came for you today," he said. He was an attractive man in his mid-thirties, she guessed, and in relatively good shape. His light brown hair was combed to one side and he was always impeccably dressed, his suits form fitting. She'd had a crush on him for the longest time and not just because of how he looked but for his intelligence. She admired him and his teachings. He was well-educated and she enjoyed having discussions with him on a broad range of subjects. It was nice to talk to someone about the topics that interested her other than her cousin.

She frowned as she took the envelope from him. She hadn't been expecting anything. Her school fees were up to date and her grades had already been posted.

"It's an art competition that I entered you into," he explained. "You're one of the finalists."

"Oh my God," she said, catching sight of the logo for the prestigious award on the letter.

"I knew you wouldn't enter yourself, though I don't understand your reasoning. Your art is excellent. You need to show it off to the world."

She blushed, her face burning. "I just don't see it

that way. I can paint perspective and have it turn out the way I want, but I don't see it to be powerful and thought-provoking, which is how I think art should be."

He nodded. "Well, I think you're extraordinary and deserve to win. Good luck."

She smiled. "Thanks, Mr. Todd. This made my day."

She continued towards the student's parking lot, contemplating the envelope. It was nice that he believed in her so much, and she would love to win, but her recent work hadn't been good, at least in her own opinion. She hadn't had a chance recently to paint, and when she did, she believed it mediocre at best.

She pushed aside her self-doubts and concentrated on how she would start her essay which was due on Thursday. Then her mind wandered to the exam coming up and she grimaced. There was so much she needed to do. Her mouth curved into a smile. Tonight she would be eating pizza. She couldn't wait. It was the one night she could goof off and gossip with Megan. School and exams were another day's problem. Tonight she would be worlds away.

Twenty minutes later, Stacey parked her late model Nissan in the designated spot in the garage of Megan's apartment building and climbed out. She shivered. The days may be warming up but the evenings were still cool and she wished she'd brought a jacket with her. She'd been in a hurry and bringing a wrap along hadn't occurred to her.

She frowned when she noticed the row of lights

closest to her were blown, casting shadows over her, but she dismissed it as she opened the passenger door to retrieve her heavy book bag from the foot well. The maintenance man would be fixing the problem shortly.

A prickle of awareness slid down her back, warning her. The hair on the back of her neck rose and she froze in momentary fear before the pain started in her lower back, reverberating up her skin. She jerked and her legs folded beneath her and she fell face first to the cold hard concrete floor.

She didn't feel the jarring impact as the overwhelming agony ran through her body. Tears burned her eyes and spilled over onto her cheeks as she breathed in years of exhaust that permeated the rough concrete beneath her skin.

She fought to move, knowing she was in great danger. But her body refused to respond to her frightened commands.

Suddenly the pressure was gone from her back and she flopped to the side as she heard the heavy footfalls step around her seizing body towards the back of her vehicle. Darkness blurred at the edge of her vision and she begged not to go under. If she slipped out of consciousness all would be lost. Her vision spun as someone carried her.

Tremors continued to wrack her body and she futilely fought against him. Her foggy brain recognised his form and strength as male. She tried desperately to scream but nothing came out.

He placed her gently down. Then, there was nothing but the darkness, but she was still awake. She knew she was. Her heart thumped out a rapid staccato. Lingering pain radiated outward from the point of impact. The electric pulsing pain made her sure she'd been hit by a stun gun.

She felt her body vibrate. Had he zapped again? When no fresh pain followed, her lethargic brain told her she was in the boot of her car and he'd started the ignition.

The bastard was abducting her. But why?

Cold shivers ran up her spine. She recalled the news article she'd seen that morning, about the discovery of another body out on the highway. Would she be the next victim? A sob rose in her throat. She couldn't die, not now. She was too young and had her whole life ahead of her. But couldn't that be said of his other victims, as well?

She tried to struggle but she'd been incapacitated and fear unlike anything she'd ever felt before chilled her body and left a metallic taste in her mouth.

"Help me," she called out, but the sound only carried to her ears.

The car bounced as her abductor drove over uneven ground, jarring her, sending fresh pain throughout her body. She gritted her teeth against the wave that intensified with every second. Tears ran freely down her cheeks and she called out again, but this time in agony, and she was almost taken under, the darkness overriding her vision. She bit her lip and tried to focus, which was becoming increasing difficult.

Megan. The name floated inside her groggy brain. When she didn't come home, Megan would immediately be alerted that something was wrong and her cousin had friends within the LAC. They would come looking for her. She only hoped they got to her in time.

Chapter 5

The autopsy had been fast. What was left of Angel Bellman's body examined, all trace evidence sent to forensics for analysing. So why was he here watching Doctor Stone cut into a dead body? The corpse was a thirty-nine year old man shot dead by his wife who he'd been abusing her on and off for the past seven years. She'd finally had enough. Dean wished he had simple cases like that. Instead, he had a serial killer—another one. While he wasn't about to say those words to the press, it was clear and it was only a matter of time before it was splashed across every newspaper in the country.

Dean had a newfound respect for his colleague Matt Murphy who'd been assigned a similar case three years ago. Thankfully, Murphy had caught and subsequently shot the man the media had dubbed the Butcher, although Dean knew Matt was still consumed with guilt over not being able to put a stop to him earlier.

Doctor Stone slipped off his surgical gloves before looking up at him. "I found the same damage to Angel Bellman's organs as I did with the other victims."

Dean frowned. Each of the victim's autopsies had shown significant scarring, almost like melting on the inside of the lungs, heart, throat, and brain. It would've been a horrific death and an extremely painful one, at that.

Stone removed his thick-rimmed glasses and retrieved a handkerchief from his pocket and promptly polished the lenses. "Whatever it is, it wasn't injected. I've searched their bodies looking for any abnormalities and the slightest pin prick would've shown up." He replaced his glasses on the bridge of his nose and regarded Dean solemnly. "It also wasn't ingested. Usually you'd see scarring in the stomach, which is not visible in this case. I've sent off samples to be tested but I'm not confident it will yield results. The body was badly decomposed and whatever was in her system would've broken down by the time she got to me."

"So we still don't know how he's killing them," Dean said. "Or why."

The weight on his shoulders intensified. These women were relying on him to bring their killer to justice. Not to mention the entire city of fresh victims ripe for the taking.

His hand curled into an impotent fist.

Stone sent him a look of understanding. "Trying to understand them is your job. Mine is just to tell you how they died. Unfortunately, we've both failed them—this time."

But how many more had to die before they found something they could use? Some days, he hated his job.

"Meanwhile, there's a woman out there, scared and alone. Trapped in whatever hell he's devised for her. I don't need to tell you the future that awaits her."

Stone's eyes darkened with rage. "I hope you catch that son-of-a-bitch soon. I don't like seeing young girls on my table."

Dean didn't like it either.

Chapter 6

Harbour Bay's LAC overlooked the harbour itself. The mud brown, L-shaped building looked as impenetrable as the Oval Office. A century and a half ago, the building had housed convicts, then sat unused until the eighties when it had been converted into the newly assigned LAC for the ever-growing police force. Freshly mowed grass surrounded the building and several trees had been planted to provide shade to the new wooden benches that had been placed about the grounds beside arrangements of vibrant, colourful pansies.

Several changes had been made since the new superintendent had been appointed, the most important being the new taskforce Amelia Donovan had founded for cases of more than one victim in hopes of limiting the causalities. Usually, Harbour Bay was quiet but as the crime rate continued to soar they tended to work cases together, combining their collective intelligence and individual skills.

Dean listened to the radio on his phone as he waited for the elevator to ascend. He was a sucker for punishment, he thought, as the public voiced their displeasure at the police. How quickly they had forgotten that the very command they were criticising had removed one serial killer from the streets not that long ago and had also taken down a major crime syndicate run by Dick Coleani, who'd nearly owned the whole damn town. The streets, while not necessarily safer, were cleaner and on their way to recovering after the constant abuse they'd received under Coleani's regime. Dean shook his head as the news reporter named him as lead detective on the Highway Dumper murders.

It was not a title Dean had asked for nor did he particularly want it. His stress level had hit the roof in recent weeks and wished he had time to knock some of the frustration out in the gym. It was the one place he could come back to—a place that held no grudges and didn't care how fucked up he was.

When he entered the command centre, everyone looked to him as if waiting for some news that would crack the case or instruction on how to proceed now that they'd hit a brick wall. It wasn't something he liked.

They were all good men and he'd worked closely with them over the years, but they began to lose touch since they'd married and started families. Matt Murphy had two daughters now, and Darryl Hill was expecting a baby any day now. He was pretty sure James Hawke would soon be joining their ranks. Dean tried to keep Nick—the only other single detective—away from women, which was proving to be difficult. The man was practically a magnet and women naturally gravitated towards him.

Dean started at the beginning, refreshing him and the others to the facts of the case. "What do we know about the victims? What links them? What makes him choose *them*? Convenience?"

Nick sat forward. "They were all brunettes around the same age."

"But not all the women had the same colour eyes or even body shape if you're thinking he's murdering one particular woman over and over," Matt Murphy added, and he was right. Each woman—while being a brunette and young—didn't share any other trait with the other victims. Their eye colours varied from different shades of brown, grey, and blue.

"Maybe the hair is enough for this guy?" Darryl Hill ventured.

James shifted in his chair so he could get a better look at the board. "None of the girls knew each other. They didn't live in the same areas or go to the same schools."

This was not the first time they'd run through the limited facts and Dean knew that each and every one of them could probably recite every case with his eyes closed. No new information had emerged with the latest body, and again they were left sitting on their arses while another woman was probably being held against her will.

"Okay then, what do we know about them as individuals?" Dean tried yet another angle to see if they could shake something loose.

Nick was the first to speak. "The first victim, Carolyn Harper, was found by the side of the highway around midnight two months after she disappeared. She'd been dead for some time."

Their killer didn't like to keep his victim's long—a few weeks at most. Was it by design? Or did he simply grow bored of them? Another possibility was that they'd angered him in some way and he'd retaliated with deadly repercussions.

Darryl sat up straighter. "I conducted the interview with the roommate. They both worked as escorts for a private company. The roommate alerted police when Carolyn didn't return home."

Carolyn's car was recovered from outside a convenience store near her home. They remained silent and when it was clear no one had anything to add, James recited the pertinent information about next victim.

"Dylan Jenkins, the second victim, was found by the highway just over a month after her disappearance. She was last seen at the strip club she worked in at three in the morning."

Dean listened to James even though he already knew the particulars. Dylan's car was taken and had since been recovered. They'd found no trace elements; the interior and door handles wiped clean. Like the other victims, her stomach revealed that she'd not eaten since her abduction and was severely dehydrated.

"The next one?" Dean asked.

James continued. "Destiny Close was found four months after she'd gone missing after taking night classes at the Uni. She wasn't a social person by nature and was living in her car to make ends meet."

31

She'd worked as a waitress at a restaurant on Maple, and when the body was discovered, the manager confirmed she hadn't shown up for her shifts for a number of weeks. Dean hated how easy it was for a person to slip through the cracks. Destiny deserved better; they all did. He vowed again to make sure the son-of-a-bitch paid for what he'd done to them.

"What about the fourth victim?"

Matt spoke up. "Jane Peterson lived on the streets like our fifth victim. Little is known about her and we've been unable to draw up an accurate timeline. Her body was the most degraded by the elements when we found her, but still held the same characteristics of the other murders—torn fingertips, starvation, and dehydration."

Dean knew how hard it must be for Matt to be involved in this case. He had an adopted daughter around the same age. Dean didn't know how the man handled himself when it came to crimes like this one when they hit so close to home. There was a reason cop marriages didn't last long, though his fellow detectives seemed to be making it work.

But that didn't mean Dean wanted to try. He'd made a deal with himself years ago that he would never fall in love. After watching his best friend die after his fiancée had been tortured and murdered in front of them, he never wanted to feel that kind of pain or be that vulnerable. Love made a man weak and he wasn't going to end up like Tony, who'd fought against their captors overseas while Dean had still been in the army. It hadn't done any good, not that he believed it would. Sweet and beautiful

Emma had been killed before their eyes even after Tony had told their captors everything they wanted to know. They were cruel men, and men like that existed in every corner of the globe.

Dean's last relationship had ended almost two years ago and even then it couldn't be called a real relationship. He liked no strings attached sex and made sure the women he dated wanted that too. Dean Matthews wasn't a man who could change, and any woman who tried was only wasting her time and setting herself up for heartbreak.

Nick frowned. "This is getting us nowhere. We can recite the facts until we're blue in the face it doesn't change anything. We still know shit. Even now, there could be another body along that highway just waiting to be found."

They all turned to Nick. He wasn't usually one for losing his cool, but this case was enough to make it happen. Women were Nick's kryptonite. He couldn't abide them suffering, least of all being powerless to do anything about it.

"What would you have us do? As you pointed out, we know shit," Dean said. "You think any of us like the fact that while we're sitting here on our arses another woman could be dying?"

The room fell into silence. They were waiting and they all knew it. Waiting for the next victim and it made him sick to his stomach.

"Let's not allow that to happen." An authoritative female voice emanated from the doorway. They all turned as their boss, Superintendent Amelia Donovan, entered the room. "I just got off the phone with a friend. She wants to report her cousin missing."

"Being a friend of the superintendent certainly has its advantages," Matt said.

"Don't you forget it, Murphy," Amelia retorted, her raven hair pulled back in its customary ponytail. She'd allowed it to grow since she'd taken office and the ends now reached her shoulders. She still looked fierce but Dean knew that would never change. She had the loyalty of every man in the room.

"And you believe this has a bearing on our case?"

"I wouldn't be bothering you if I didn't, Matthews. Stacey fits the criteria." Amelia handed Dean one of her business cards and he saw the hastily written address on the back. "I'll let Megan know you're coming. Be gentle with her. She's a wreck right now."

Amelia turned and left the command centre. Dean knew she wanted to be there to ease her friend's suffering, but she'd given that up when she'd accepted the role of superintendent. Dean didn't kid himself. Amelia would be riding his arse from this point on. She'd wanted him to close the case before to protect future lives, but things had just gotten personal.

Chapter 7

Following Nick out of the elevator, Dean started towards apartment 3G. The building was only a couple of years old and well out of his price range. The hallway was a deep chocolate brown and the lush, carpeted floor a merle grey. Everywhere he looked screamed opulence. What type of woman could afford a place like this?

A warm golden glow came from the rectangular wall sconces spaced a few feet apart, lighting the hall without blinding the occupants. At either end of the hallway stood a pair of identical leafy green potted plants. A bronze framed print hanging on the wall reminded Dean of Picasso.

The apartment three doors down had their music blaring, and beneath his feet he could feel the vibrations from the bass. Everything seemed so normal—so pedestrian it was hard to think they were here to investigate the abduction of a nineteen-year-old girl. They came to a stop in front of apartment 3G and Nick knocked. The door was opened immediately by a petite brunette who

35

must've been waiting for them.

A pair of startling green eyes caught his and Dean felt like he'd been kicked in the gut. His heart thumped heavily in his chest as little pin-pricks of awareness washed over him and he found he had trouble breathing. His muscles tensed even as his body hardened and began to throb painfully. He bit back a curse. He'd never had such a reaction to a woman before in his life.

Her gaze flicked between him and Nick as he brought up his I.D. and made the introductions. The woman nodded and stepped back, allowing them to enter. She closed the door firmly and turned to face them, her expression fraught with worry.

"I know who you are. I just got off the phone with Amelia. She told me you'd be coming," she said, twisting her fingers together anxiously. When she caught him watching, she stuffed her hands into her snug jeans. "I'm Megan Bailey."

He gave her a slow onceover, unable to help himself. He was curious about this woman and the overwhelming desire he had for her. The entire world seemed to melt away until all that was left was her.

She was beautiful in an understated way with a honey complexion and a small dusting of freckles on the bridge of her nose. Rich mahogany hair had been pulled back into a messy ponytail. She wasn't overly tall, the top of her head only reaching his shoulders, but she was nicely filled out with curves in all the right places, her breasts high and full beneath her shirt, which clung to her like a second skin revealing her tucked in waist and the flare of her hips. He swallowed hard, his mouth suddenly dry.

As if sensing his perusal, Megan glanced over at him and his knees weakened. Her eyes—those gorgeous emerald pools—pulled at him, so full of torment that his heart ached. Shit, this was crazy and so unlike him.

She blinked and he heard her sharp exhale, her mouth parted, and she looked so irresistible that he was sorely tempted to cross the short distance between them and find out if she tasted as good as she looked. He was at a loss, unable to pull away as she continued to stare at him. Was she feeling as out of control as him?

He forced himself back on track. He was here to work a case, not look for his next bed partner, and while Megan was quite delectable, she would hardly do. She wasn't the type of woman a man fooled around with unless he had forever in his mind, and Dean Matthews didn't do forever. No matter what his body was telling him.

He certainly wasn't sex-starved, although it had been a while since he had hit the sheets with a woman. The case was taking up all his time, and he couldn't think of anything else even when he had a rare moment alone to sleep. It was disconcerting and he wasn't sure he liked it, bringing about feelings he'd long ago rejected.

Nick shifted where he stood and Dean remembered they weren't alone. He looked away with effort and caught Nick's knowing glance, so he scowled at him in return. Great, he'd witnessed his less than subtle once over. He'd be hearing about his reaction to Megan for days. Nick winked at him before turning towards Megan.

"How do you know the boss?" Nick asked—probably idle curiosity on his behalf, but the question was designed to put her at ease.

Her shoulders visibly relaxed and she cast Nick a wry smile.

"I'm a writer. I called your office a while back asking to speak to someone about police procedures for research on my first book, and I guess it was supposed to be a joke, but I was handed over to Amelia."

Guilt crossed Nick's face. Dean guessed he'd probably been involved in that decision. He was the perpetual joker, and when Amelia had been a part of the team, he'd loved to bust her chops.

Nick studied her. "And you managed to become friends?" It was a fair question. She wasn't the warm and fuzzy type, and like the rest of them, her schedule left little time for building a relationship—any type of relationship.

"It took some persuasion on my behalf to get past that prickly exterior, but once I did, we hit it off."

That was hard to swallow. No one just *hit it off* with Amelia Donovan. Although Megan was right about the prickly exterior. Dean had worked alongside her for years and the only things he knew about her was that she was passionate about her job, had a wicked aim when it came to pitching stress balls at him, and that the closest thing to family she had was her previous team and their wives. But then, Dean wasn't much for sharing, either. He'd never told anyone what he'd endured overseas and how watching Emma die had fucked with him.

The memory of Emma had the effect of ice water being poured over his head. She was a good reminder of why he should retain a good distance away from this woman who was messing with his head, making him feel all sorts of things that he shouldn't. He couldn't afford to lose focus, or another woman might end up like Emma.

"So you're a writer," Nick said. "Anything I might've read?"

Megan shrugged. "Probably not. I write under the name Meredith Baker."

"No? Really? *You're* Meredith Baker?" His eyes rounded. "I love your books. I've got the entire series and between you and me, I've fantasised about Dahlia Blake more times than I can count, although I prefer redheads."

Dean's eyebrow rose. He had no idea Nick read, let alone what he assumed to be a woman's romanticised view of police work.

She glanced between the both of them. He froze as their gazes collided and he tried to remind himself of all the reasons he'd just told himself to stay clear of her.

"Thank you. I'm glad you liked them—and her."

"I can't wait for the next one."

Megan looked uncomfortable under Nick's enthusiasm. "Well, you'll be happy to know I finished the next one yesterday and it was handed over my editor for review."

"Please tell me she's going to put Cole out of his misery and marry him? They're so right for each other," Nick said. "Dahlia will never find another man who understands her and accepts her like Cole does."

Dean rolled his eyes. Romantic nonsense. But he found himself curious about the characters in her book and was surprised at how hooked his partner was. His mouth twitched.

Megan smiled at him, clearly as amused by Nick's rapture as he was. His gaze drifted down to her lips and when he glanced back up, he caught the blush staining her cheeks before she ducked her head.

"I wouldn't want to spoil it for you. But since you're my biggest fan, I'll make sure you get an advance copy."

Nick placed a hand over his chest and sighed dramatically. "You certainly know your way to a man's heart, Megan."

Her face suddenly fell as if she'd only just remembered what they were doing in her apartment and tears pricked her eyes. She hugged herself tightly as if that alone would bring her comfort. Dean wanted to take her into his arms and hold her until she no longer hurt, but he wasn't that type of man. He wasn't someone to be relied on for sweet lies and false hope. He was a man of action and the best thing he could do for her was catch the man who'd taken Stacey and bring her home. Hopefully alive.

Nick laid a gentle hand on her shoulder as a tear escaped her eye. Dean was surprised at the anger that rose within him and barely restrained himself from reaching over and forcibly removed his partner's hand. Dean frowned, feeling inadequate and pissed that he was unable to provide comfort. It seemed to be so natural for Nick, but Dean knew if he tried, it would come off as awkward. Emotions weren't his forte, which was why he preferred other people deal with the grieving families while he dealt with the facts and evidence.

Why was he so incapable of reaching out to another human being and making a connection—any kind of connection other than the sexual? Just because he'd long ago denied himself certain feelings, it didn't mean the rest of the world had. What was it about seeing someone so vulnerable that had him wanting to find the nearest exit? He already knew the answer. It brought back too many memories of when he'd been defenceless.

Megan apologised. "For a moment it wasn't all bleak, and then it was like discovering her missing all over again. It's like a nightmare. I keep expecting her to walk through the front door."

"It'll be okay." Nick patted her shoulder reassuringly.

Dean directed her attention to him. "Stacey lived here with you?"

"Yes. She's staying with me while she attends HBU. I'm her only relative besides her mother."

"And where does her mother live?"

"A couple hours west of here. I've already called her, hoping maybe Stacey made contact. But she hasn't heard from her in months and all I got out of it was her berating me for not taking better care of her daughter."

Dean didn't think the mother needed to tell

Megan she hadn't done a good enough job. It seemed like she was doing a pretty good job of blaming herself.

"Her name?"

"Cathy Bailey."

Nick studied a photo on the wall. "Is that Stacey?"

"Yes."

Dean glanced at the photo. At first he thought he was looking at a younger Megan, but then he noticed a few small differences. The chin was sharper on the girl in the picture and her smile was lopsided, unlike the rare one he'd seen on Megan's face.

He removed the picture frame from the hook. "Do you mind if we borrow this?"

"No, go ahead." Megan stepped forward and he breathed in her jasmine scented perfume. Her eyes locked on his and he felt the same pull as he had earlier. "Amelia said this wasn't a ransom, so what exactly *is* it?"

Dean shared a look with Nick. Thank you, Amelia. Way to throw them into the deep end. He tried to be diplomatic. "We don't know yet, Ms. Bailey. As soon as we have some answers, we'll let you know."

"You know something now don't you? How else would you know it's not a ransom? It's not a—" She broke off and tried again. "He's not a sex—" Again, she couldn't finish.

Dean kept his gaze steady. "No, Ms. Bailey, we can say with absolute certainty that he does not want that from your cousin."

She sucked in a startled breath. "You know who it is?"

He realised his mistake. "We need a list of everyone your cousin comes into contact with. Friends, lovers. Everyone." He ignored her question.

Megan looked lost again. Dean breathed a sigh of relief. The last thing he wanted was for her to make the connection between the Highway Dumper murders and Stacey's abduction, although it was only a matter a time. He hoped he would have some answers for her first.

"Stacey isn't much of a social person. She's driven. Her studies are what's important to her at the moment. I don't think she's made any friends. I don't think I've ever heard her mention anyone from Uni, except maybe her art teacher."

"Well, you also have to understand that she might not have—"

"Stacey tells me everything. I know what you're going to say...there are some secrets a teenage girl has, but there's no reason for Stacey to lie to me. She knows I won't condemn her or rat her out to her mother. She's an adult and I treat her as one. I'm not her mother, her conscience, or the moral police."

He understood what Megan was telling him but the jaded part of him still believed teenage girls didn't tell the authority figure in their life everything, even when that person was a cool older cousin.

"Ms. Bailey, is it all right if we go to Stacey's room and look through some of her things?"

"Yes, of course. This way."

They followed her down a hallway and for the first time Dean glanced about the apartment. It was a woman's apartment. There was no mistaking the smell of clean linen and sanitised benches. No socks littered the floor nor were any clothes thrown about. He walked past an open door and spared a glance inside. It was Megan's room clearly, the large queen bed covered with a feminine comforter. He could smell the vase of flowers on the bureau emanating from the open door.

They came to a stop out the front of a closed door and Megan opened it reverently. The room was just as clean as the rest of the apartment but there were several items of clothing left discarded on the floor.

Megan watched them from the doorway. She looked like she was scared to enter the room, as if afraid it might mean Stacey would never come home.

Dean flicked through her things, feeling like a voyeur. He wasn't used to shifting through a live person's belongings. It made what he was doing intrusive somehow, despite his best intentions. He found little evidence of a life outside her studies, as Megan had said. There were no emails on her laptop besides upcoming exams sent out by the university, no photos on either the computer or about the room that weren't of Stacey and Megan.

His heart filled with dread. For a time, he'd been hoping that maybe the kid had simply taken off, but now it seemed more than likely that she had been taken by the very man he was searching for. The knowledge that she was out there, in the hands of this monster, made it so much worse. She was in great danger.

She was so young. So unprepared for the hell she was about to endure. He wished he could take her place. He was used to pain, had been trained to withstand it. He couldn't be broken. He hardened his resolve, refusing to give up on her. Ever.

He flicked through a folder on her desk and scanned the detailed business ideas, price projections, and loan repayments for an art gallery. He smiled. The kid had certainly done her research.

"She's going to call it Bailey's Art Gallery," Megan said softly, and he turned his head, surprised to find her so close. How had he not heard her, not sensed her approach? She stood beside him looking down at the folder in his hand.

"Is she? She certainly has a good business plan."

"She's studying business at school. Stacey's a good kid. Do you honestly believe this will end well, Detective?" Her voice broke.

Dean opened his mouth but stopped when she held up a hand.

"Honestly," she repeated, a cold steel in her voice.

Dean dragged a hand through his hair. "I have no idea, Megan." Her name slipped from his lips before he could stop it. "I wish I could provide you some comfort. But that's not who I am. God, I wish it was. We'll find her. I promise you. No matter what, I'll bring her home to you."

Her eyes widened at his vow. Hell, even he was surprised to hear those words come out of his mouth. He'd made a point over the years never to put himself in this position. Never personalise the case. But he just couldn't remain aloof this time. He was vested in the outcome just as much as she was, and accepted that if all went to hell, Megan would end up hating him.

He caught Nick's disapproving stare in his peripheral vision. He ignored his partner and focused on the woman beside him. A lone tear trailed down her cheek and he caught it with his finger. The simple touch sent a bolt of electricity through him. Megan startled, sucking air in sharply. Her eyes widened and she stared at him in wonder.

Nick cleared his throat and Megan blushed. She stepped towards Nick who was waiting not so patiently at the door, holding Stacey's laptop in his hands for the IT techs to scour.

"I'll have my editor, Riley, send you a copy of the book as soon as it's printed, Detective Doyle. I'll even sign it."

Nick's voice was full of hope. "'To my favourite detective'?"

Dean scowled at him and Nick winked. Bastard was purposely baiting him. He gritted his teeth.

"Sure."

Dean followed her to the door. "If you have any questions, please give us a call." He handed her his card.

She took it. "But you'd prefer it if I don't?"

Dean smiled at her directness and had to give credit where credit was due. Megan Bailey was smart and very astute. She also seemed to be the bottom line kind of woman. Dean appreciated that.

Chapter 8

Dean stepped into the hallway, Nick following closely behind him. Megan Bailey wasn't at all what he'd expected. She'd blown him away and he wasn't comfortable with the power she seemed to have over his body, still feeling the lingering effects in his trousers. He pressed the call button on the lift and waited for the carriage to arrive. Nick rocked back on his heels, a wide grin on his face.

"Can it," he warned, his voice low and dangerous.

The man always ignored his warnings. "I haven't said anything yet. I seriously never thought I'd see the day Dean Matthews fell hard for a woman. Hell, you were *comforting* in there. At least as much as your awkward arse can. Guess we know who's next."

Dean scowled at him. It was a running joke within their team. Years ago when Matt had married Natalie, he'd turned to them and said they were next. Like a curse, one by one, they dropped until it was just him, Nick, and Amelia left.

47

"I guess you're human after all." Nick was unrepentant as he followed Dean into the elevator.

Dean turned the tables. "What about you? I heard there was a blonde in the picture."

He vaguely remembered hearing Nick talk about a blonde he was seeing. There was some secret to her. Nick rarely elaborated on his relationship. Why was that? He was usually an open book, and if he was infatuated, everyone knew about it.

He didn't miss the way Nick tensed.

"I did. Vanessa. We broke up."

"Mutual, or you broke up with her?"

"It couldn't have been her, right?"

"No, all the women seem to want you. I can't imagine any of them giving you up voluntarily."

"Yeah, you're right about that, this one certainly wanted me. A little too much."

He left it at that. Dean knew there would be more to the story, but decided against asking or pushing. If he wanted to talk, he'd talk. Certainly not before. He, like the rest of the detectives in their unit, kept things close to the vest, especially when it was important. None of them liked being probed. They were a close knit team, a makeshift family. They shared their lives, but some things were just plain private.

The elevator came to a stop on the ground floor and opened to a richly furnished lobby. A door on the right led to the stairwell and to the left were a bank of mailboxes. Despite the expensive surroundings, there was little security around Megan's building, which surprised him. The front door was open to the public, but at least there were cameras that fed back to the front desk.

They stepped out into the fresh spring breeze. It was late—almost one am—and Stacey had been missing for over six hours. Had she not fit the victim's profile, he would've thought she'd taken a much needed break from her hectic school life. But she did fit the profile, and that scared Dean more than anything.

"What do you make of her? Despite the obvious," Nick said as they made their way to Dean's car, parked across the street. "I'm never getting the image of you eye-fucking her out of my head."

Dean grumbled under his breath.

Nick chuckled. "You should read some of her books. There's this one scene where—" He grinned. "Never mind. I don't want to spoil it for you. But let me describe it in one word...hot. I wonder if Megan would be interested in getting a male perspective on the Force."

Dean pinned him with a hard look. "Stay away from her."

Nick raised an eyebrow. "She's not a person of interest, is she? She's an adult...I'm an adult. What's the problem?"

"She's a vulnerable woman."

"As if I'd take advantage. What do you think I am?" He sounded irritated.

Dean sighed. What the hell was wrong with him? He knew his partner was the last man on earth he should be lecturing. If there was one thing Nicholas Doyle didn't mess around with, it was women. "My apologies. I know you're not that type of man."

"You're jealous," he said, awe in his voice. "You actually think that given a chance, Megan would choose me over you. Let me tell you something, Dean, she barely knew I was there tonight. She only had eyes for you. Besides, I missed my chance."

Dean frowned when he realised Nick had diverted the call Megan mentioned earlier to Amelia.

How had Nick survived this long without Amelia decking him? Hell, Dean was an extremely patient man. Years of being in the army had made him that way, but sometimes even his patience grew thin and the need to plant a fist into his cocky partner itched at him. Some days, Nick could be extremely trying. Other days, he was a fantastic detective. Truth be told, he was the light of their team, while the rest of them often moved about in the dark, their seriousness overwhelming.

"So are you going to make a play?"

"No."

"Why not?"

The list was longer than his arm. He didn't want Megan to be hurt and he knew he'd damage her one day if they got involved. He couldn't have that on his conscience. She'd been made to smile and laugh. Dean wasn't. He'd seen too much horror. He wouldn't bring Megan down to his level.

"I think you're making a mistake," Nick said.

"I don't recall asking you for your opinion."

"You're getting it anyway. And if you hadn't spent the last ten years of your life trying to forget, you would know when to take a chance. Megan seems like a good woman. Who knows, maybe she could put up with your shit."

"What do you know about my 'forgetting'?" His jaw clenched, the words like acid on his tongue. He was a private person and he didn't like to think that Nick had been profiling him. His past wasn't something he wanted advertised.

"Hey, we all have things we'd rather forget. Horrible things that cause nightmares. But do you know how you fight a nightmare?"

"With a bottle of Wild Turkey," Dean half joked. He'd done exactly that more than a time or two.

"No, with something nice, something pure that drives away the nasty image. Stop fighting, Matthews, you can't live your life alone. Sometimes you need someone to lean on, someone to hold, and believe it or not...someone to hold you."

The image of Megan holding him deep into the night made his body warm in a non-sexual way. She could probably drive away the nightmares, but at what cost to her? Dean knew without trying that he would end up alienating and even pushing her away.

The past was very much in the present and it wasn't something he could just easily let go of. He needed the reminder because it kept him alive, and he was strong because of it. He didn't want to hurt, didn't want to be betrayed or have his heart broken, and Megan could do that if he let her. He knew it wasn't something she'd set out to do, but the possibility was too real to ignore.

The best thing would be to keep his distance. Reduce the exposure and temptation. He had what he needed from her, at least regarding the case.

There should be no reason to contact her again until they found Stacey.

Nick let out a sigh. "Seriously, you need to read her books. I'll lend you my copies. Romance and sex. You can't go wrong."

Chapter 9

The door closed and Megan pressed her forehead to the cool wood, her body feeling hotter than she was comfortable with. Pressing a hand to her stomach, she stepped back. What the hell just happened?

Megan rolled her shoulders but her muscles remained tense. Whether from the situation or Detective Matthews's overwhelming presence, she couldn't be sure. Both seemed to dominate her thoughts simultaneously.

He'd looked at her as though he would devour her. The fierce expression sent a thrill zinging through her bloodstream. Her heart only now appeared to be slowing down. She couldn't say what it was about him, but her pulse thrummed from his nearness, her stomach a swarm of butterflies. Had he also experienced the unexpected attraction? Hot and swift, almost knocking her down with its intensity, her knees weakening at the promises she'd seen in his gaze.

At least she hoped that's what she'd seen. Being

desired gave her a confidence boost. She could write all-consuming romances, yet she hadn't lived one, making her feel like the world's biggest hypocrite. Still, how nice would it feel to be held within the comfort of his arms? She thought of how they'd been highlighted beneath his shirt in delicious detail.

She shook herself. Now was not the time to be contemplating a hunky blond. Stacey was out there somewhere, alive. She couldn't believe otherwise.

Holding on to hope, instilled within her by the hot detective with warm, chocolate eyes, she prepared sweet tea, her nerves rattled.

Why would anyone want to hurt her cousin?

Megan would not give up. Someone had the answers and she was prepared to beg, borrow, and steal to get Stacey home safe.

Her hand trembled as she raised the cup, tea spilling on the counter, scolding her fingers where they hugged the warm porcelain.

Cursing, she wiped away the spill, feeling the tears welling in her eyes, unable to stop herself from sobbing.

How could she have let this happen?

For as long as she lived, she would never forgive herself. It was her job to take care of her cousin, to keep her safe, and she'd failed miserably.

Now she might be suffering horribly. The images her thoughts provoked had her falling to the floor, unable to remain standing as the weight of her despair pulled her down.

Weeping uncontrollably, she buried her head in her hands, her shoulders shaking.

Her phone rang, cutting into her misery. She shifted, hiccupping as she forced herself to move, hope blossoming inside her. Stacey. Whoever had her would find no resistance in Megan, and she would gladly give them everything she had. Heart pounding, she snatched her mobile from the counter, her recent elation plummeting when she read the call I.D.

"Don." Her voice mirrored her emotions as she answered. Dark. Harsh.

She wasn't about to pretend it hadn't affected her. Even if she could bother, Amelia Donovan would call her on her bullshit. Her breath stuttered.

"I knew I shouldn't have sent Dean," her friend said. "He's a good cop but his delivery sucks. I'd hoped Nick's presence would have counteracted Dean's abruptness. I'll skin him alive," she added, sounding irritated.

Panic overtook her fear. "No. Don't. It's not him. He was—"Wonderful? Kind? "Gentle. I just...it just hit me. I'm so scared, Don. What if I don't get her back?"

"It'll be okay."

Will it?

She chewed on her thumbnail, feeling vulnerable and needy. She desperately wanted to believe both Amelia and Detective Matthews, to cling to the reassurance in their voices. It wasn't easy, knowing with each passing moment that the chances she'd see Stacey alive dwindled. She needed to do something, anything but sit around waiting to be told the worst words imaginable.

She wanted answers, needed to know her cousin

was okay. The waiting was too much, eating away at her nerves.

"Dean's the best. Truly, Meg. I wouldn't have sent him otherwise. Let him do his job. Don't get in the way."

Megan smiled. Sometimes she forgot how well Amelia knew her.

She sniffed and tugged a tissue free from the box nearby. She blew her nose before crumpling the used paper into a wad inside her fist.

"I promise." She fell silent again, feeling comforted that Amelia, while not in the room, was with her in spirit. Sounds of her busy office filtered through the line. Megan's heart constricted. Amelia must have her own hell to deal with, yet she took the time to ensure Megan wasn't a step away from an emotional breakdown.

"Why Stacey, Don? Why her? I just don't get it."

Not that she'd wish this torment on anyone, but Stacey was a good kid. So quiet that sometimes Megan forgot she was there.

She didn't expect an answer. If her friend knew why, she'd have caught the bastard already.

Rubbing her palm over her throat, she said what was in her heart.

"I failed her, Don. I didn't keep her safe."

"Stacey will not see it that way."

"I do."

A few minutes later, she disconnected, allowing Amelia to finish her work. There wasn't anything more she could do or say to alleviate the pain rocketing through Megan, but knowing her friend was there helped. Her back stooped as she rested her arms on the counter. Staring at the phone, Megan willed it to ring. For Stacey to tell her she was safe. For the nightmare to be over. But she already knew it had only just begun.

Where are you, Stacey?

Chapter 10

Stacey had screamed until she was hoarse before succumbing to loud, bone jarring sobs. Her throat was raw and each breath was painful. She was scared, her body cold with fear. Her heart beat erratically and she feared it would give out. Her limbs shook uncontrollably, not from cold, but from bone deep terror.

Her bladder had already given out hours ago. She was embarrassed and ashamed at having had to relieve herself in the corner of the room like an animal or risk soiling her clothes.

The room was bare, void of anything except a blanket and pillow on the floor. She could smell the laundry detergent her captor had used on the fabric. It smelled of lavender and sunshine. How long had she been missing? Time held no meaning to her and there was no way to track it. Surely, Megan had discovered her gone and had called in the cops?

Her stomach growled and she rocked her body back and forth, wishing she could be anywhere but here. She wanted to go home to her quiet life with

Megan.

She hadn't seen her captor, hadn't spoken with him, had no idea what he wanted from her—what he wanted to do to her. That frightened her the most. It seemed as if she'd fallen asleep and got caught up in one of her cousin's novels. The darkness surrounding her threatened to swamp her and the stillness of the room was slowly driving her insane. Her mind was her only escape, so she closed her eyes and created a world of fantasy where she wasn't alone, wasn't scared. She was on a deserted island, lying in the sun, a mimosa in her hands. She could feel the UV rays kissing her skin, her mahogany hair lifting in the breeze and could practically taste the wetness of her drink on her lips, trickling down her throat. She groaned.

Already she could feel her heartbeat returning to normal, her fear temporarily pushed aside. She smiled, determined not to let him break her. She would survive. She moved her mind away from the island, returning it slowly to the room. She had built a map of the room in her head, detailing her position and any possible weaknesses. She had already searched the room for her bag or her school supplies and had found nothing.

She was still wearing the same clothes, but there was nothing she could use as a weapon or a tool to escape. On her previous examination of the room, she had discovered only brick walls, the scent of freshly paved concrete assaulting her nose.

No door. No window. Nothing.

She had to find a way to escape. She couldn't rely on the police to find her. She remembered the articles she'd read. If she was correct, she had been taken by the Highway Dumper. He'd been killing for months and was still at large. She bit back useless tears, fighting to hold on to her composure. She was going to need every brain cell if she planned to get out of her dungeon alive.

Chapter 11

Dean took a sip of his coffee, the hot liquid burning his tongue and filling his bloodstream with much needed caffeine. He'd hadn't slept in over thirty-six hours and had no plans to in the near future. After leaving Megan's apartment two days ago, they'd returned to the LAC where they'd met with the rest of the team to go over what they'd learned. Unfortunately, that hadn't been much.

Stacey's online presence was limited—surprisingly so for a girl of her age. She had a Facebook page with only a handful of people as supposed friends, and most appeared to be students at the university whom she'd been study partners with. Her cousin was also listed, but he'd refused to look at Megan's page. He didn't want to know more about the woman who was already occupying too much of his mind. Despite the decision he'd come to, she was still dominating his thoughts.

He pinched the bridge of his nose as he reviewed the case. Stacey's last known sighting had been on the school campus, seen by several students talking with one of her professors. He and Nick had tracked down Jason Todd down and questioned him. Dean had disliked him on sight. The pompous man looked down on them as simple cops, which annoyed Dean. He got the sense the man believed they were lacking in intelligence because of their chosen careers.

Dean was used to the misconception despite knowing his IQ was probably on par with the professor's, if not exceeding it. But he had nothing to prove, and continued to question the professor until they'd locked down a timeline which was corroborated by several others.

Yet, still, the knowledge they discovered didn't help much.

Next, they'd shifted through Stacey's financials to see if she'd ever visited the same venue as one of the other victims, but she only had one student credit card and used it for school books and fees. Her bank account showed a regular meagre deposit from her inheritance left to her by her musician father, but other than her car and a few items every now and again like clothes and shoes, she never spent anything, and never beyond her budget.

Her browsing history showed research for her essays and even her business. Stacey had bookmarked several blogs where people shared their experiences in the business world and how they'd dealt with certain issues that arose.

It seemed her one true passion was her dream, and Dean could easily envision a Bailey's Art Gallery on Commerce beside the wharf where Dick Coleani's five star restaurant had once stood. Stacey had the type of personality that could make water into wine. She would succeed; her high grades told him that. She was acing all her classes and he could easily see why Megan was so proud of her cousin.

Which was why he'd been surprised at her mother's attitude. He'd called Cathy Bailey earlier that morning to ask a few questions about her daughter. The woman had ranted and raved about Megan, saying she never should've let Stacey live with her. She called Megan an immoral, loose woman.

She'd even asked him if he'd read any of Megan's books, and when he said no, she described the plots, going into detail about sex scenes and how it wasn't right to publish that kind of smut. Now, he knew he'd have to take Nick up on his offer and borrow some of those books. When he'd gotten her back to the subject of her daughter, the woman had admitted she knew nothing about her life.

The last contact Stacey had initiated had been via email, which was backed up by her laptop. The contents concerned the exams she was taking, as well as her grades. There was nothing in the email about personal life outside of school. Obviously, Stacey knew what her mother wanted to hear, and told the rest to Megan.

He leaned back in his chair. Megan had been right. Stacey's mother did not approve of their life choices. Her daughter was an adult, yet she still wanted to command her. It was clear why she'd chosen to live with Megan. He wouldn't have wanted to live with such a woman, either. Dean was glad his parents had supported him no matter what. They hadn't opened their arms to embrace his career choice, but they hadn't been disappointed in him, either—nor did they push him into something he didn't want.

Intrigued by Cathy Bailey's earlier comment, he hadn't been able to stop himself from researching the woman who'd given Megan life. Mara Craven had been as different from Cathy as night was to day. From all reports, she'd been a groupie—the kind depicted in *Almost Famous*. She'd been nineteen when Megan Leigh Bailey had been born, and she'd toured with her husband and brother-in-law across country for the first eight years of Megan's life.

From the few websites dedicated to the small fan base of The Baileys, it was said that Mara and Liam had a Courtney Love and Kurt Cobain kind of relationship. His heart melted at the pictures posted of a young Megan with her parents. She looked like her father but had the same intelligence he saw reflected in Mara's eyes, who it was said home schooled her daughter until she was nine. She'd then been enrolled in a regular school as Mara stayed at home to help her sister-in-law deal with her new baby after having post-partum depression.

Megan's mind certainly hadn't suffered. He clicked on the official website of Meredith Baker. A picture of a smiling Megan was the first to catch his eye. It was a candid shot, and she stood in front of a large gum tree, the sun shining on her hair, revealing red tones. He recognised the setting as a park in Harbour Bay. Her eyes twinkled with happiness that matched the diamonds making up the letter *M* on her pendant, which sat just below the hollow of her throat. She was easily the most beautiful woman he'd ever met and his body responded painfully. He reached down and adjusted himself in the tight confines of his pants.

He flicked through her website, knowing his time was better spent elsewhere but unable to close the window. He read her bio, noting very little personal information, only her professional career and the awards she'd won. He soon found himself at the section listing her books, glancing at the enticing covers that drew the reader in before they'd even read a word. He clicked on the excerpt of her first novel and was sucked into Megan's world, richly painted with words and intrigue.

When he was done with the excerpt, he found himself downloading the complete novel to his PC and continuing on, drawn into the sexy world of Dahlia and Cole. He could see why Nick liked it and why she was one of the most popular authors in the country. She was quickly becoming his favourite, and he'd read the finest novels ever written—a perk being the son of an English professor.

Nick stepped up to his desk, a folder in one hand, a water bottle in the other, startling him. He'd been engrossed in the novel and hadn't heard him approach. He quickly minimised the window containing the book, silently telling himself to send a copy to his phone later so he could continue reading when he wasn't in such a public place. After his reaction to Megan the day before, the last thing he needed was for more ridicule sent his way for reading what could be considered a trashy romance novel. Although, it was the farthest thing from trashy.

Dean looked over at his partner as he drank heavily from the bottle. They'd caught a break when one of their patrol officers had located Stacey's car abandoned down by the beach. Nick had volunteered to ensure it was safely transferred back to the LAC so that forensics could catalogue any evidence while Dean returned to the office. The tie around his neck was loose and beads of perspiration coated his forehead, a clear sign of the heat of the day. "Shit, it's getting hot out there. Have you seen the high today? It feels like the dead of summer out there. I almost damn near dived into the surf while waiting for the tow truck."

While living on the coast sounded nice, and was for the most part, it sucked for those who couldn't make the most of it. He couldn't even remember the last time he'd headed down to the beach for a swim or even a BBQ. The team had gone for Matt's birthday one year, but that was pre-Natalie and the kids, so it had to have been at least four years ago.

"I assume the car was wiped down?"

"Yep." Nick attempted to air out the damp armpits of his shirt. "There was no blood in the car, but the forensics boys did find Stacey's hair in the boot."

Dean's eyes narrowed. "He stuffed her in the boot?"

He was lucky he hadn't suffocated the girl, rendering her unconscious and placing her in a confined space with limited air. He could only imagine what it would be like to awaken in a dark, small space, not knowing where you were.

"It looks that way." Nick glanced towards the Command Centre.

Dean had already added the timeline of Stacey's day from what they'd gathered from several sources and now had a pretty clear understanding of when she'd gone missing. Darryl Hill was now in the process of tapping into surveillance cameras around the school, Megan's apartment, and the possible route she'd taken home—if she'd even made it that far. It was tedious work, but it might prove lucrative.

"I'm going to head down and take a shower…unless you need me to do anything?"

Dean shook his head, and soon heard Nick's footsteps fading away as he headed towards the elevator.

Moving into the Command Centre, which was empty for now, the rest of the team off completing the tasks he'd assigned them, he rubbed the back of his neck. They hadn't yielded any results that would crack the case, yet. It was slow and frustrating. His gaze drifted over each of the victim's photos, wishing he could do more. It was a waiting game. He was frozen until the next key piece of evidence was found. He hated that. Especially knowing there was someone suffering because they'd yet to find this guy.

A startled gasp filled the silent room and Dean spun around to find Megan staring at the corkboards, her eyes filled with the horrid, graphic photographs of the victims and crime scenes. Damn. It was a sight she'd never forget.

"Megan, you shouldn't be in here."

"Oh my God. What is all this? Is…is that what's going to happen to Stacey?" He caught her stare and was floored at the torment in her eyes, the condemnation. His stomach twisted painfully. He reached out to drag her from the room, away from the horrible sights, but she jerked away and he felt her rejection acutely.

***

Megan stepped away from him. Up close, he was very formidable, large enough to make a woman think about how vulnerable she'd be should he use his strength against her. Not that Detective Matthews would. She sensed he'd die for a woman before allowing anyone to hurt her—at least physically.

She focused on him like a lifeline, anything to keep from looking back at the images now burned into her memory. He faced her, his expression made from stone, any emotion hidden from her gaze.

"I'm not going to allow that to happen Megan."

Another vow. Another he couldn't possibly keep, but there was conviction in his tone.

He hadn't quite lied, but he'd withheld several key facts. Her heart hurt. It was stupid to feel betrayed by him. She barely knew him and he'd made no promises to her, except to bring her cousin home.

Her brain had been foggy with equal parts of

overwhelming desire for him and concern for Stacey, but once he'd left, she stayed up all night because she couldn't sleep, replaying their meeting over and over again in her mind. After about the fifth time, she realised he'd never really answered her question about the man they believed had taken Stacey. Her mind wouldn't allow her to forget and the words spun around her head until she'd craved peace. Now she was regretting her rash decision to storm into the LAC and demand information. She felt defeated the moment she caught sight of those terrifying photos.

Then there was her insane attraction to the extremely sexy man before her. A man had never affected her like this, because no one lived up to the characters in her novels—especially the men.

She'd fallen in love with her hero, but failed to find a man in real life who could compare to Cole...when suddenly Detective Matthews had entered her apartment.

Tall with thick, muscular biceps and a hard, broad chest, he was every woman's fantasy.

His chocolate eyes focused on her with an intensity that made her shiver, goose bumps appearing on her skin. Her body responded in a way that made her want to take her clothes off. She was acutely aware they were alone, and it was crazy. It seemed with each passing minute she was becoming more aware of him as a man. A very hot, delicious, sexy man who smelled sinfully good. His scent was a mixture of man and the outdoors—wickedly erotic.

Her skin tingled as she remembered the way his

eyes had practically devoured her the last time they'd met. Her mouth felt dry at the memory. It seemed as if every time she'd looked at him, he'd been watching her silently. There'd been a spark that raced through her bloodstream at his touch—a simple touch of his finger to her cheek. She was dying to know what it felt like to have his hands on her naked skin, particularly her breasts. Her nipples hardened into taut beads at the thought.

She shouldn't even be thinking this way. He was hell on her concentration, not to mention her libido. She felt like a complete bitch for once more forgetting Stacey was missing. By the look of those pictures, she was in grave danger. She snapped her attention back to the point of her visit. Information. She wanted answers, needed to know her cousin was okay. The wait had been eating away at her nerves. Her mind conjured up the worst possible scenarios, the corkboard wall only adding to her nightmares. She refused to allow herself to cry, because it never helped.

"So it's true. The same man who has Stacey also did this." She didn't take her gaze off his, intending to take note of any hesitation that might indicate he was lying—and also because she didn't need to see those photos anymore.

"We believe so. She fits his profile. Young. Brunette. A loner."

Her breath caught in her throat. "Who is he?" Unable to control the tremor in her voice, she knew it broadcast her fears. She raised her hand and rested it against her throat, toying with the diamond *M* necklace she always wore. Stacey had bought it for her birthday years ago.

"I take it you haven't seen the news lately?"

Megan frowned. "No. I just finished a novel. When I'm writing, I live in that world with those characters until that reality ceases to exist for me. I'd even forget to eat if Stacey didn't wake me up to feed me."

"We call him the Highway Dumper. He's killed five women that we know of."

Feeling lightheaded, her whole world seemed to crumble around her. A piercing ringing filled her ears as tears flooded her eyes. She tried to blink them back, but she couldn't stop herself, making her feel even worse—emotional and out of control.

A feeling she didn't like.

"You lied to me." She snapped the words, instantly wishing she could take them back.

A sob escaped her throat. Desperation consumed her and she spiralled toward a full-on emotional breakdown before turning on her heel and storming out of the conference room. Her vision swam, she barely avoided stumbling into a desk on her way out. She jabbed her finger on the button for the elevator, hoping the detective wouldn't follow her.

The elevator arrived and she stepped inside, turning around so she could hit the right button to send her to the ground floor. Disappointment filled her when she found herself alone. As much as the idea of facing him after her outburst embarrassed her, being alone felt worse. But what could she expect? She'd just blamed the man for something he wasn't guilty of. He may have promised to bring Stacey home, but he'd never said alive. She was the foolish one to assume. She should've known better. A seasoned detective would've known better than to promise anything.

Megan wished she'd left well enough alone. It was bad enough knowing some deranged man had her cousin, but it was worse knowing what'd happened to the women who went before her. Now she felt horrible. Detective Matthews had been protecting her, shielding her from the truth for as long as possible, allowing her to live in a fantasy world of hope. One she'd been all too willing to surrender to. Now the illusion was shattered and she only had herself to blame. On top of that, she'd been a bitch to the one man who'd been kind to her.

Megan's shoulders shook as she sobbed silently, ducking her head from view as the door opened to a surprised group of people waiting for the elevator. She scurried out of the LAC and raced blindly to her car.

Chapter 12

He watched her pace the floor, much like a caged animal plotting against its captor. She was a smart one, more so than any who'd come before her. She'd already scoured the walls looking for vulnerabilities, but she was wasting her time. There was no escape.

It excited him when they were scared and screaming for help. He fed off their fears, liked feeling powerful because he controlled their lives—their fate.

It pleased him to see her there, at his mercy. Much as he'd been at her mercy, for years. He hated her, yet he also loved her, but now it was time she was punished just as he'd been.

His hand curled into a fist.

She hadn't expected him to improve on her method. She'd been fantastically horrible at inflicting pain, but she'd been simple-minded in her torture. He touched his scarred face, a physical memory that would stay with him forever. He'd been lucky not to lose sight in his right eye.

Yet, he still loved her, and it was difficult to separate that from his hatred.

His captive continued to stare at him, defying him. She refused to give him what he wanted, what he needed. She hadn't shed a tear, hadn't raged. Instead, she'd calmly surveyed her prison, and it unnerved him even though he knew there was no way she could get out. He'd tested for vulnerabilities and found none.

Maybe she wouldn't do at all. He got no joy from her, and soon she would no longer entertain him. He'd dispose of her just like all the others.

As if sensing he was watching, she turned and glared up at the camera he'd mounted on the wall. Her anger towards him was evident. He sat forward, watching her stare into the camera with defiance. His mouth twitched. She was a strong one.

He would enjoy breaking her.

Chapter 13

"I'm sorry," Dean blurted out the moment Megan opened the door to her apartment. Her eyes widened at seeing him there and she immediately wrapped her arms comfortingly around her body. His heart ached. "I handled it wrong. It wasn't my intention to keep the truth from you. I just wanted answers to give to you."

Her gaze softened and she nodded before standing aside to allow him to enter. She led him into the family room off the entrance through a wide arch, where he was met with warm rich tones, uniquely female. The room was comfy but not cluttered and the furniture was new, having only been bought in the last few years, the fabric maroon and the wood dark stained. But there was one piece that caught his eye—a large well used recliner that looked good enough to sink into with a moan. A small table on wheels sat beside the chair and a laptop rested on top, ready for use.

In the corner of the room beside the rectangular window on a stand, resting upright was a 1963

Fender Stratocaster, the ash body with a double maple and cream top finish. Had the guitar once belonged to Liam Bailey, Megan's father?

There were no ornaments about the room, only several sweet smelling candles and paraphernalia that women tended to collect. A bookcase filled with reference books, photo albums and a cornucopia of paperbacks took up one wall on the right. Mixed amongst the books were several framed family shots. Dean recognised a recent photo of Megan and her cousin.

A few older pictures lined the shelves, one of two men, and for a second Dean thought the man was standing beside a mirror but on a second glance he noticed the men were twins—Megan and Stacey's fathers, perhaps? That could explain the similarities between them.

Beside it sat a candid shot of Megan with her parents. She'd been about four at the time, he guessed, and it was clear the family loved each other. For some reason his heart twisted. She'd been adorable, not that she wasn't now, but looking at someone's past always gave him insight.

The smoky red walls held two large prints, both oils, the first overlooking the bay from Kent's Point and the other of the wharf from the perspective of someone sitting on the dock. They'd both been expensively framed, but Dean couldn't make out the signature of the artist.

The dark slat venetian blinds were closed, blocking out what he assumed to be a dazzling view of the city. The apartment complex had been built in a prime position, and the real estate hadn't been cheap, the residents either opting for the water view or the bright lights of the city. Soft cream carpet, probably more comfortable than his own bed, covered the floors. Should he take his shoes off? Megan wore a pair of clean sneakers. He decided not to worry; he wouldn't be staying long enough for it to make a difference. He shouldn't even be there, but he hadn't been able to get her out of his thoughts. She'd looked so devastated that he'd wanted to chase after her, but he figured his presence wasn't wanted.

She took a seat in the large recliner.

"I'm sorry too. Your job is hard enough without me barging in and accusing you of keeping secrets. I know you wouldn't be as forthcoming with me if I wasn't Amelia's friend."

He held back the denial that rose to his lips. Let her think that, because it was easier that way. No need for her know he wanted to ease her suffering.

"I didn't lie to you. I meant what I said. I'm bringing Stacey home to you."

He wanted to be clear on that fact. As much as his instincts warned him not to promise something he may not be able to deliver, he needed to give her hope. Needed to offer reassurance like he needed his next breath.

Her eyes filled with something he couldn't name. No woman had ever looked at him like that, but he liked it. He wanted her to trust him. When he thought he'd lost that, he'd been shattered.

Her head bobbed, her gaze downcast. Did she think he was simply giving her a line?

"Do you believe me, Megan?"

She swallowed hard but didn't look up, focusing instead on his chest. "Yes, and I know you shouldn't be promising me such things, and I thank you for all you're doing for my cousin."

He wished he could do more. He hated sitting around waiting, wondering if the next call he got would be about her body being discovered.

"Do I have something on my shirt?" Self-consciously, he shifted as she continued to stare at the watermelon coloured shirt he wore.

Megan bit her lower lip. "No, it's just—"

"Not very masculine."

"No," she agreed.

"My ex started the trend by buying me one. I didn't want to upset her at the time." He hated his entire wardrobe, but his masculinity had been questioned and Dean never backed down from a fight. Now it seemed even sillier to have worn every froufrou shirt in existence because of the taunts he'd been subjected to, mostly by Nick. That man had always been able to irritate him.

Megan met his eyes. "An ex? That's very—"

He held up his hands. "Don't say sweet," he warned. Megan seemed the kind of woman who gushed over puppies and went out of her way to play matchmaker. He didn't want her to think it was anything more than male pride that kept him wearing pastel colours.

"Well, whoever she was, she didn't know you very well. The colouring is all wrong for your skin tone. No wonder she's your ex."

"I bought this shirt."

"Oh…sorry." Megan looked away, a blush rising

from the collar of her black blouse.

"It's all right. Fashion was never one of my strong suits."

Megan gave him a bright smile and his heart almost stopped. He could get used to that sight. He immediately squashed the thought, realising he was in enough trouble already.

So why wasn't he leaving? Why was he not in the gym working up a sweat? What was it about this woman that intrigued him? He studied her, beginning at her size sevens, moving up her long shapely legs outlined beautifully in denim, her curvy waist, full high breasts and those gorgeous emerald eyes, hidden behind long dark lashes, her face framed by a thick mane of mahogany hair. He'd have to be dead not to see the attraction, but it wasn't just her body that beckoned to him.

Dean eased down on her coffee table, the oak wood directly in front of her chair. His long legs reached across the small space, his knees bumping against the recliner. His legs touched hers as he rested his hands in his lap. "Tell me about Stacey."

She raised an eyebrow. "What more can I tell you, Detective?"

"You'd be surprised. Describe her to me...not as a victim, but a proud cousin."

"She's intelligent, smart as a whip, kind, caring, and sweet. She's also stubborn and pig-headed and knows what she wants."

"Her gallery?"

"Yes. Everything she's doing now is in preparation for opening her business."

"You're very proud of her. A shame her own

mother isn't." He winced as he heard his own words. He'd not meant to voice his opinion.

"You spoke with Aunt Cathy?"

He inclined his head.

"I take it she had some unfavourable things to say about me. To her way of thinking, I've led her daughter astray. I never understood what Uncle Damien saw in her, but I suppose love is blind and stupid."

"What of your own parents?"

"My mother was wonderful. Smart and beautiful. She loved my father very much. He was her only downfall. She died within two months of his death, unable to live without him."

That information was in the file on Dean's desk. He couldn't imagine loving someone that much. Never felt the compulsion to, either. It wasn't as if his parents didn't love one another—they did, but they were academic people and they just didn't understand such deep passion. Life went on, and all you had to do was pick up the pieces.

How would Matt react if something happened to Natalie? Would he embrace what life dealt him, or join his lover? The same went for Darryl and Kellie, and James and Aimee. Or were they all jaded, having dealt with the harsh light of day for so long they took what they could while they were still able? He sent her a self-deprecating smile.

"Let me guess…you want a relationship just like that. Is that why you're not married, why there's no man here comforting you?"

Her shoulders rose and fell. "You're here, and that's enough for me."

He sat listening as the round wall clock ticked. It wasn't an uncomfortable silence, more a companionable one. A slew of emotions crossed her face as if she was working through some inner turmoil.

"I don't want to love someone so much I can't live without them. It's selfish. Don't get me wrong…my mother loved everyone, but she would walk over hot coals for my father. No one should ever have that kind of power over another human being."

Surprise rocketed through him as he heard his own thoughts spoken in Megan's voice, her lips forming the words he had decreed so long ago.

A knock sounded at the door and Megan shot up from her seat suddenly, tripping over his legs and stumbled into him, almost landing in his lap. With a quick movement, he steadied her, his hands on her hips. He felt her heat and breathed in her floral scent, his gaze falling to her breasts, and for a moment he watched them rise and fall. His breathing became ragged and he fought against pulling her astride him where he could feast on her luscious body. He gently pushed her away and on unsteady legs she moved towards the entrance. Dean followed her and leaned against the wall of the arch, just inside so he wouldn't be easily noticed. He frowned, his jaw clenching when she opened the door without looking through the peephole first.

"Oh my God, Megan, I am so sorry." A woman's voice carried into the apartment. Megan stepped back from the door, allowing the woman to enter, her sky blue blouse untucked from her black A-line skirt, and her red hair slipping from its tight confines. She embraced Megan and squeezed her hard in comfort, then stepped back, keeping hold of her shoulders. "Why didn't you call me?"

"You're busy. I didn't want to disturb you."

An inelegant snort filled the room. "The moment I don't have time for my friends is the day I don't deserve them. You're family, Meg, don't you ever forget that. You can count on me for anything. Even if it's burying a body or bailing you out of jail," she said jokingly. "So what's being done about this? We have to get Stacey back, even if I have to march down to the LAC and light a fire under their arses myself."

Dean raised an eyebrow, immediately liking Megan's redheaded friend. She had balls.

Megan glanced at him and the woman followed her line of sight, a blush staining her strawberries and cream complexion when her gaze found the badge clipped to his belt.

Dean straightened, holding out his hand. "Detective Dean Matthews."

The woman cleared her throat as she took his hand. "Riley O'Neill. I'm Megan's editor and friend."

Dean looked down—way down. Riley O'Neill was small, her head only reaching his breast bone. He had several inches on her, and she was wearing heels.

"Megan has some good friends."

"She deserves them. I'm sorry about those comments, but I've known some cops in my time who can be extremely lazy and unfortunately they give the entire force a bad name."

For a moment, he was intrigued to know why the woman had been in the company of cops, but then the interest faded. "I've met them too, but me and my team are doing everything we can to bring Stacey home safe."

Riley seemed appeased by that. "I just don't understand how this could happen. Stacey is a wonderful girl with a bright future ahead of her. Why would someone want to hurt her?"

When she looked at Megan, Dean guessed she saw what he did. While still pretty, she looked tired, almost ready to collapse. Riley reached out, rubbing her palm gently up and down her friend's back, offering what little comfort she could.

Dean's palms itched to do the same. He stuffed his hands in his pocket.

"Unfortunately, it doesn't take much to pop up on someone's radar."

"Believe me, I know. A lot of crime novels pass my desk. I've read every motive under the sun, but it never changes. People will always hurt one another…it's their nature."

Dean liked Riley more and more with each moment. It was like his life had been overrun with strong independent women who were capable of running the world. He admired those women. His own mother was one of them and never let him or his father forget it. It was her, Georgia Matthews, who made professor first, and got herself a cushy job at the University. Now, she oversaw her entire department. His father had been the one to remain obscured in the shadows, but Dean knew he didn't care. He did what he loved and that was enough for him. He took his wife's accomplishments in stride and was the first to celebrate.

"As it's in their nature to complain and even threaten," Riley continued. "They're just not content without some semblance of violence in their lives."

Dean frowned. "Has Megan gotten any threats?"

Megan wrapped her arms around her body again, hugging herself. She'd been quiet, lost in her own thoughts for the past few moments. He was amazed she was able to keep up with the conversation while living in her private hell.

"I had one recently that gave me shivers." She caught his gaze and held it. He stopped himself before he acted on his urges and leaned towards her.

"No writer is immune, and unfortunately, the higher success rate, the more you become a target for fanatics and fans alike. Not everyone likes a good romance, Detective, and you don't always find critics in the paper, they're your average housewife and strangely enough middle-aged men." Riley squeezed Megan again. "You should read her books. They're quite inventive. Even you would be surprised."

"Maybe I will." He didn't mention he'd already started. What he'd read so far was enough to keep him in suspense, practically dying to turn the page to continue—and he would have, had he not been interrupted by Nick and had a case to solve. But by God, he would finish that book. He was particularly interested in reading the bedroom scenes. *Hot and sensual* was one comment he'd read on her website. *Sizzling and tantalising* was another.

"You don't have to." Megan's gaze focused on him. "You're not exactly in my demographic."

"Neither is Nick," he countered. "And he seemed to enjoy them all the same."

Her mouth curved. "Yes, true, but I figured you for more of a true crimes kind of guy. Mine are purely fictional."

Dean shrugged. "I'm diverse."

"So, Detective," Riley began, and Dean knew what was coming, her tone of voice speaking more than her. "What *is* being done to find Stacey?"

"Riley." Megan's tone held a warning.

He found he liked her concern.

"It's all right, I'm a big boy. I can handle any questions, no matter how difficult or uncomfortable they may be. We currently believe Stacey was taken by the Highway Dumper."

Riley paled and swore. Dean's mouth twitched. The woman could've easily been a sailor in a previous life.

Megan studied Riley's reaction. "You know who that is? You're worse with keeping current than I am."

"Michelle keeps me up to date. I can't believe it. The Highway Dumper? Are you sure?"

"She fits the profile." Megan recited the same words he'd said to her several hours ago.

"Whatever you need, you've got it—okay, Megs? Anything at all."

"Thanks. That means a lot to me."

A phone went off and Riley rolled her eyes

85

before answering her mobile. Dean heard a frantic tone on the other line.

"Michelle, relax, you can do this. Just pull yourself together. I need you to do this for me. I'm needed elsewhere tonight."

Megan caught hold of Riley's wrist. "It's okay. Go do what you need to. I'll be fine, really."

"No, you come first. Michelle just needs to put Hollows in his place."

"Oh, Riley, you can't leave Hollows up to Michelle. He'll eat her for breakfast. Go save your assistant, she needs you more than I do right now. I'll be fine. Besides, I have Detective Matthews here with me. He isn't done questioning me yet."

Riley appeared uncertain, but she huffed out a sigh and told her assistant she'd be there soon.

"You're a good boss."

"Not really. I was the one who stuck her with Hollows's new book launch." She hugged Megan goodbye before holding up her mobile. "I'm just a phone call away. If you need me, just call, and I'll drop everything."

"I know. Thank you."

Riley glanced at Dean. "I want to do anything I possibly can to bring Stacey home safely." She reached into her purse and pulled out a white business card. "My numbers. Call me if you have a question, or if I can prove helpful in any way."

"I will, Ms. O'Neill, I promise."

Chapter 14

Dean closed the door. Megan slipped into her kitchen, situated off to the left with its smoky quartz benches, obsidian black cabinets and rich rosewood floor. A bowl of various fruit rested beside a stack of unopened mail on the nearest bench where two stools sat under the overhang. Dean glanced appreciatively at her heart-shaped bottom.

"She's—"

"There's a lot of energy in that small package and a lot of brains too," Megan said. "I've seen her take down men twice her size and come out picking their bones out of her teeth with her fingernail. She can be frightening, which is why I'm glad she's on my side." She switched on the coffee maker. "Coffee?"

"No thanks." Dean sat down on a stool. "Tell me about Megan Bailey."

She glanced up from measuring out the coffee, surprise etched on her face. "No more Stacey?"

"We'll get back to her, but you're just as much involved in the case as she is, and I want to know more about you."

It was the closest to the truth that he'd ever admit, which was why he wanted to dissect her life, not just for the case but because he needed to know and understand everything about her.

Soon, the room was filled with the sounds of the percolator. Megan placed her arms on the kitchen counter and leaned towards him. From his position he could see right down the gap of her tank top and at the two creamy globes that greeted him. He forcibly raised his chin and locked his gaze on her face, ignoring the tempting view.

"I had quite the unconventional childhood." She picked at her nails. He noticed her thumbnail had been chewed into a jagged edge. "I never set foot inside a classroom until I was nine. My father was a musician and we followed him from town to town. Did you know I won my first literary award when I was eleven?"

Dean shook his head.

"It was called *Tour Girl* and it was about a young girl who toured the world with her famous father, only she manages to get caught up into a high profile criminal case. In the end, she foiled the bad guys' plan just in time to watch her father play." She smiled at the memory. "It was a ridiculous, childish story."

"It couldn't have been that bad. It set you on your path."

"No, I have my mother to thank for that. She was extremely intelligent, always expanding her mind. She surprised many people who believed her to be a simple roadie. They were always underestimating her, but she proved them wrong. There was a brilliant brain inside her head. My mother tutored me. She was determined my education wouldn't suffer because of our nomadic lifestyle and had me constantly constructing stories, making use of the English language in all its complexities."

"She sounds like an amazing woman."

Megan smiled, warming his heart.

"She was. What about you, Detective? How did you end up as one of Harbour Bay's finest?"

"We were talking about you."

"We were…and now we've moved on to you, temporarily. I'm extremely curious about you, Detective."

His heart thumped. She couldn't mean in the way he hoped, but the words still affected him. Much more than they should have.

"Not much to tell. There's not much work for an army man, at least one who wants to remain active in the field."

"Yet, you chose to serve your community as a government man rather than in the private sector."

"It was never about the money."

"Which is what makes you special, Detective. The kind of people I write about—a real hero. You might not recognise it in yourself, but others do. I do. You care about those around you, those who are taken advantage of, who can't fend for themselves."

His face heated. He wasn't used to such praise. He cleared his throat. "You were telling me about yourself."

She appeared to examine his expression for a moment. "I embarrassed you, didn't I? I'm sorry, and you're right, we were talking about me. From a young age, I was blessed with the ability to tell a story of distant lands, magical places, and knights in shining armour. Nothing was too grand or wild or beyond belief. The sky was the limit. Stories just came alive in my head. My mother encouraged me and fed my mind with the classics, even the books you'll never see on a shelf, ones long forgotten."

He grinned and ran his fingers through his short hair, his fingertips brushing against his head. "My mother would like you."

Megan frowned. "Why is that?"

"Because you're the very embodiment of everything she's ever wanted. She's spent her life collecting and preserving books. Like your own mother, she consumed every written word she could get hold of. It was hard being the only kid in primary school who'd devoured every Shakespeare play, or Scott and Dickens novel in existence."

His mother had ensured he'd not grown up ignorant and he knew words that could probably rival Megan's extensive vocabulary, but he didn't like to flaunt it. Besides, he rarely had the opportunity.

Megan's enthusiasm was clear. "I'd love to meet her some time, discuss her latest find. Although I doubt I'd be of interest to her. My novels aren't exactly going to stand the test of time like Austen or Alcott. But that's okay, because it's not why I do it. Not to sound conceited, but I want to share my vivid imagination with the world, or at least that's my dream. Right now I'm working from the east coast to the west, but one day I'll get there."

"I don't doubt it. You are a strong-willed woman, and like Stacey, you'll get what you want in the end."

"You make that sound like a threat or a promise." She straightened. "It's hard. As a writer, everywhere you look you see a story developing. You hear something and the next minute you have a plot sitting in your head. Hell, even my dreams are narrated like a book."

"I wasn't complaining. I like it. It's sexy,"

Oh shit, did I just say that? Sexy? Great, now she knows. But from the moment they met, he hadn't been able to take his eyes off her. She'd probably already realised it.

"Uh—"

"It's all right. I know. You think I'm sexy." She blushed, turning away.

She was teasing him, and she wasn't very good at it, either. It was obviously as alien to her to tease as it was for him to receive. He couldn't remember the last time any woman had teased him.

They stood staring at each other for several long minutes, and the urge to take her in his arms was strong. He found himself gravitating towards her tempting lips. His gaze locked on to what he assumed was satiny soft flesh. Her tongue swept out, moistening the pink, well sculptured lips, leaving a glistening trail behind as it disappeared back inside her mouth and Dean almost groaned aloud, the need to possess the sweet heaven they provided almost urgent.

He leaned forward, focusing on Megan, aching to know what she felt like. Was her flesh resilient or soft? Did she taste sweet? Would she come apart in his hands? His body hardened with the images and he jerked back, just inches—seconds away from entering a zone he could never return from. She wasn't like the other women he'd had. She wasn't a one night stand kind of girl, and he would hate himself for making her feel anything less than perfect.

Dean pulled back, angry with himself for what he'd almost done.

She wiped down her counter before looking up at him. He shifted under her gaze. Was she aware of what had almost happened? He doubted it.

"Can I ask you something? Would you mind staying here with me tonight? Please don't feel obligated. It's just that I've never realised how quiet this place was without Stacey and the silence is deafening. I'd rather not be alone if I can help it."

His instincts told him to say no and run like hell, but the earnest look on her face had him caving.

"Sure. It's not a problem."

"Thank you. I appreciate it."

She rubbed her hands over her bare arms as if suddenly cold.

"You don't mind staying in Stacey's room? It'll be more comfortable than the couch and she won't mind."

She looked away but not before he caught the glistening tears in her eyes. She remained quiet while she fought for composure.

He clenched his jaw. He couldn't stop himself, and he pulled her into his arms. She melted against him, her hands sliding around his waist, her head resting against his chest. He breathed in her vanilla scented hair and tried to ignore her lush body so close to his. The last thing she needed right now was feeling his desire for her pressed against her stomach. This was about comfort, something he didn't hate as much as he thought he would.

"Thanks." She stepped back. "I needed that."

He dropped his arms. Was her voice slightly husky due to holding back the flood of emotions coursing through her? Or had she been as affected by the embrace as he was?

He felt like an arsehole to be thinking of sex when it was clear she was upset, exhausted. Dark circles marred the creamy skin beneath her eyes, making it clear she hadn't slept a wink after his last visit.

"You should go to bed. You look like you could use a good night's sleep. I'll be here if you need me."

She was pure temptation, so close that he didn't think he could resist.

Her nose wrinkled. "Is that a polite way to say I look like shit?"

Panic flared inside him. He wasn't good at this at all. He'd meant to be kind and compassionate, yet had ended up insulting her.

His thoughts must've shown on his face as she chuckled.

"It's okay. I know that's not what you meant. And you're right. I think I'm still standing on sheer will. Good night."

She started off towards her bedroom before turning to look back at him over her shoulder.

"It helps, you know. You being here. Thank you."

He nodded, unsure if he could trust himself. She was seriously doing a number on him.

She disappeared into the bedroom. The soft sounds of her undressing reached his sharp ears. When he heard her settle on her bed, he followed her down the hall, noting she hadn't closed her door. A quick glance into the darkened room told him she was burrowed deep beneath the blankets.

He slipped inside Stacey's bedroom and closed the door, needing that barrier between them.

The room felt eerie, hitting him where it hurt most. He should've been able to catch this bastard by now. But he wasn't any closer than he'd been ten months ago when he'd originally been assigned the case.

It was his fault she was missing and he couldn't stop the images of the other women from entering his head. Only, this time, it was Megan's face he was seeing.

A shiver ran down his spine. He hoped that wasn't a premonition of things to come.

Chapter 15

Stacey wondered if she'd leave the empty room alive. She knew someone was out there looking for her, knew Megan would be doing everything she could to find her. Her cousin could be hell on wheels when she wanted something, and would run over anything in her way.

She envisioned her issuing orders and demanding action, knowing she'd use just about anything at her disposal to make sure she was found. She'd call in favours from her friend the police detective, and wasn't that woman in charge now? She had no doubt people were searching for her.

She moved slowly away from the sleeping bag, her body stiff from the concrete floor beneath her. She barely made it upright before she was bending at the waist, her stomach contracting as she dry-heaved. Her eyes watered from the effort or from the smell emanating from the small space. In the hours or days since she'd been here, she had to relieve herself many times and her strength was quickly waning.

She'd already expended too much energy working well past the time her body wanted to rest and sleep, urgency pushing her on, a part of her knowing it was all coming to an end very soon. She'd located the only structural vulnerability in the room—an amateurish and not well cemented brick wall which she hoped and prayed was covering the exit. Hope was a dangerous thing, because it could either make or break her.

The wall before her wasn't like the others, as if the cement hadn't had time to dry. She hoped she could use that to her advantage, and spent what seemed like days scraping at the small centimetre of concrete between the bricks with the plastic end of her shoelaces. When they broke, she moved on to the buttons of her blouse, her earrings, hair clip, and she'd even removed her jeans to use the finger tab of her zipper.

The backs of her hands and fingertips were scraped and bleeding. But even in the dark, Stacey knew she was close to being able to remove a brick and had chosen the loosest one she could find. Her hand quivered in exhaustion and pain as she attempted to get fingers into the hollowed out groove and dislodge it. Tears fell down her cheeks but she didn't give up. She cursed a couple times, yet remained calm. She'd lasted this long without going insane, so what was a little while longer?

She gritted her teeth as she felt the brick move just a little bit. Or had she imagined it? She took a deep breath and continued to try. A moment later, it gave way, popping out of formation and into her lap. Elation flowed through her and she almost fainted, the darkness coming so close she'd swayed before regaining her equilibrium. She didn't give up easily.

Stacey grabbed at the next brick and yanked hard. It didn't take much time after that to remove a small square a woman her size could fit through. Her breath lodged in her throat as the section she'd freed gave way to a doorknob, and with one good smack with a brick, the knob came off, bouncing loudly on the concrete floor.

Stacey listened for a moment, wondering if her exertions had been overheard. She had no idea what time it was, and no light appeared as she pushed open the door and began to crawl through the small section of missing bricks. Her stomach scraped along the jagged edges and sharp bits of concrete and she swallowed her cry. She was so close to escaping. Where was she? Was she still in Harbour Bay or somewhere else entirely? Was she in a house or an old barn? Were there any neighbours close by or was she in the middle of nowhere?

Images from the movie *Wolf Creek* played across her mind and not for the first time did Stacey wish she'd never watched the bloody film. She was scared enough as it was without that kind of imagery bouncing around her head. The coolness of wood panelling met her palms as she reached out to the ground on the other side of the door. It felt like heaven to her, and as quietly as possible, she moved her body to join her hands. When she was completely free of her small dungeon, she evaluated her options, looking around the darkened room. It was night, and she saw the bright moonlight shining through white lace curtains.

Stacey blinked, working out the layout in her mind and orientating herself before turning to what she assumed to be the front door. She would've preferred going in search of a phone to call triple 0, but didn't want to risk running into her captor. Outside, a dog barked in the distance and she breathed a sigh of relief. A dog nearby meant she wasn't as far away from civilisation as her overactive imagination had assumed. She crept along the floorboards slowly, not wanting to run the risk of making a noise. The house seemed older, maybe built in the seventies if not earlier, and the sounds of the foundation settling gave her the creeps.

Straining her eyes to see in the darkness, she reached out, grabbing hold of the doorknob, her free hand searching for the lock. She gently unlocked the heavy deadbolt before slowly twisting the knob, the slight *click* sounding loud to her.

Her body shook with the effort it took to take her time, her brain crying out for her to make a run for it, and she would as soon as she could open this door. She pulled the door ajar. In an instant, a shrill alarm sounded, and the panel beside her lit up like a Christmas tree. Her bladder gave out, dampening her jeans. For a frozen second, she stood there, scared into motionlessness at the repercussions of the sound, and then all of a sudden her brain began to function again. Her feet moved, picking up speed as she ran through the doorway, down a pebbled path and slate driveway. She didn't bother looking back, didn't dare to check whether she was being followed. She desperately sought out a neighbour or a dwelling in which she could seek refuge.

The ground beneath her sneakered feet crunched, her lungs burned, and she was sweating profusely as she ran. Her heart raced as she moved away from the road, not wanting to be seen. She'd read somewhere that roads and rivers were the easiest way to track a person, the human body sticking to what it thought it could depend upon. Rivers and roads usually led to help. The night air was warm, the breeze cool on her hot body as she began to slow down, wanting to give up the fight.

Stacey powered on, her gaze vigilant as she started to make out the trees and bushes surrounding her. Her foot caught on a root and she stumbled, her body crashing into the hard ground, knocking the wind out of her, bruising her already injured body more. Stacey laid in the dirt, stunned, her body aching, the sounds of night animals surrounding her. She couldn't move, not even when she tried. Her fingers curled into the fallen leaves and other growth beneath her.

Her heart stopped when she heard the sound of footsteps and she bit her bottom lip to keep from whimpering. She hoped she couldn't be seen; she wasn't exactly hiding, but surely he wouldn't be looking at the ground for her. She wished she had the strength to pick up a stone and throw it far away from her, hoping to lead him away. The dog barked into the night, followed by a growl, obviously sensing her danger and wanting to do something about it. A moment later, a man scolded the dog, telling him to get back inside and leave the possums or foxes or whatever the hell he was barking at alone. She couldn't even risk calling out to him. Despair curled its ugly fingers around her and held on tight.

No, please, Stacey cried silently. *Don't leave me. Please let the dog out of the yard, let him come find me. Help me.*

A sob welled up and she almost choked on it. She closed her eyes in an effort to calm herself. *Go to your happy place, Stacey,* she told herself. *The sun, the sand, the beautiful blue ocean. Can't you feel the humid breeze and smell the salty surf?*

When her body relaxed, she reopened her eyes and stared up at a dark gaze burning in the centre of a silhouette, and she knew she was beaten.

Chapter 16

Megan rolled over and struggled with the tangle of sheets, trying unsuccessfully to sleep, but whenever she closed her eyes she either saw Stacey suffering at the hands of an unknown man or a sexy arse detective sleeping in the room down the hall. She'd already imagined several delicious scenarios: Dean taking her on the bed, her legs tightly wrapped around his hips. Her riding him hard until she drained him completely. Closing her lips around him and sucking him into her mouth, tasting him.

She was a mixture of turned on and scared as hell. It was disconcerting. Maybe she was a little sex deprived. She blushed, remembering how she'd imagined fucking this man she hardly knew as if she was some insatiable whore.

Was he having similar problems knowing she was so close? He hadn't acted like spending the night had been a chore or a pleasure. But he was on the job and she was the emotional relative of a victim. Perhaps he was a gentleman and wouldn't take advantage of a distraught woman. Which was probably a good thing. Megan wasn't sure she'd deny any advances and if she was going to have sex she wanted it to be because of mutual attraction and not some misguided attempt at comfort.

Frustrated, she unwrapped herself from her bedding and wearily rubbed her hand over her face. She climbed out of bed and shivered as the cool early morning air touched her skin.

She had no idea what to do. Usually, if she couldn't sleep, she'd read or even plot out her next novel but her concentration was shot.

She stopped in her doorway and leaned against the jamb as she glanced in the direction of Stacey's room. She could hear the detective's soft snoring and it oddly soothed her, filling her with calm. A strange feeling.

How did Dean and his co-workers manage to deal with such events day in and day out without it affecting them?

But maybe it did. They were human, after all, and there was no cure when they saw the remains of a child or another such brutal case. How did Dean deal with it?

He probably didn't. He didn't seem the type of man to talk about his feelings, to let anyone know he was weaker than he looked. Maybe that was why he was so stiff all the time. The horrible things he must've seen—it was a wonder he hadn't gone crazy.

Just thinking about the things that *could* be happening to Stacey was making her insane.

She stretched, and with it went her need to sleep. Her body felt wide awake as if it was ten in the morning rather than five hours earlier. She hated it when sleep eluded her, when she couldn't turn off her mind. Usually, it was a good thing when she was in the midst of writing a book. The best parts came when she laid down in the dark and let her mind soar.

Megan stared down at the mess that was her bed, then collected the knotted sheets from the floor and piled them on her mattress. She turned towards her door, not sure what to do as she stepped out into the hall.

***

Dean heard Megan's footsteps in her bedroom. His well-trained hearing picking up the slightest sounds. What was she doing up at this hour? He pressed the button on his watch, illuminating the face, showing the time. He hadn't been able to sleep, not due to his new surroundings or the fact he was sleeping in a teenager's bed, but because Megan was just a few feet away.

Her warm body was so close to his.

How could he be expected to think of anything else, let alone sleep? His heart began to pound as he heard her approach the door, and a light knock sounded right before she opened it. Dean sat up, clad in the undershirt and slacks he'd worn to bed. "Megan, what are you doing up?"

"I couldn't sleep, and when I saw a light from under your door, I wondered if you were awake too."

She must've been watching the door. His body

103

warmed and he struggled to swallow. "I'm an early riser. My shift starts in a few hours."

"I just wanted to say thank you. For everything. I know you've gone way beyond the call of duty and I appreciate it."

If there was one thing he *didn't* want from her, it was gratitude. Not that he could allow anything to happen between them. She was part of the case he was working, and although the rule had been broken many times before by his fellow teammates, he had no intention of joining their ranks.

He liked knowing she was off-limits, that he had an excuse to keep her at a distance. If he let her, she would crawl right into his life and turn him upside down. If he believed she wanted a one-nighter and could trust himself to keep it that way, he wouldn't be lying in the cool bed alone right now. But it wasn't about Megan at all, it was about him. He knew he'd want more than one night with her.

Shit. She was already under his skin, and worst of all, he'd allowed it. Dean was always so careful when it came to women. No one woman was ever his partner, and he played the field—not to add notches to his bedpost but to keep everyone at a distance. He had no intention of ever caring for someone so deeply it would kill him to lose them.

"The boss wants you to be looked after," he said, keeping his tone impassive.

"Oh." Was that disappointment he heard in her voice?

Amelia would expect them to watch out for Megan, but the truth was, he was going out of his way to ensure her sanity.

"Well, still…thank you, Detective. I'm sure even with Amelia's orders, you do what you want to, and if you're here…it's because you want to be."

Dean raised an eyebrow at her perceptiveness. She was one sharp woman. Yet another thing he liked about her.

"You're welcome."

Megan moved closer and he shifted self-consciously on the bed. His eyes had adjusted since she'd arrived, and he could see she wore very little. A pair of shorts revealed long legs and her shirt didn't conceal the fact she wasn't wearing a bra, the cool air hardening her nipples into stiff peaks. All he could think about was taking one into his mouth and sucking on it. His dick swelled painfully and he ached to give himself some relief.

He took a shaky breath. They were treading on thin ice. She sat down on the bed beside him and her gaze searched his.

"Promise me you'll not keep me in the dark. That the moment you hear anything, good or bad, you'll tell me."

"I thought we went over this. You can trust me, Megan. I was a fool to try to keep the truth from you, but it was done with the best intentions."

She took his hand in hers and squeezed. "I know, and I do trust you. But not knowing is killing me. Please, you can't protect me from the pain."

"I promise."

"Thank you."

He wasn't sure what to say. He was in way over his head and had no idea how to save himself. He wasn't even sure he wanted to. Megan stood and her hand skimmed over Stacey's belongings reverently.

"When will this be over? I'm so scared. For her. For me. Life can change so quickly. All it takes is a second. A blink of an eye. A beat of a heart." She turned to him. "Before I came in here, I was wondering how you dealt with all this on a regular basis. What it must do to you. You're a remarkable man."

He was a damaged one. The weight of his past was heavy on his shoulders.

"I'm no hero, Megan. Don't go painting me as one," he warned. "I'm human just like everyone else. Flawed. Scarred. I'm going to disappoint you, Megan. That's another promise."

His phone vibrated on the table beside the bed, sounding loud in the quiet room. He silenced the alarm he'd set, thankful for the interruption.

"I'm sorry," she said, standing. "I'll let you get ready for work."

Dean almost asked her to stay, but in the last second held back and waited for her to depart before he pulled on his button-up shirt and finished preparing to leave.

Chapter 17

Riley looked up from her desk at the looming figure of Kenneth Johnson. She raised an eyebrow at him as he stood leaning over her desk, glaring at her. She glared right back. Over the years, she had learned to deal with men like Jackson, men who thought they could push their bulk and strength around. Riley had learned not to back down, not to give in and to fight fire with fire and had gotten very good at it. There were very few people who weren't intimidated by her. She knew never to back down. Never bluff, just in case she was caught.

She'd been hurt badly years ago, enough to bruise and leave scars, but it was something she kept to herself, a secret that not even her family— her older brother Declan—knew about. She wanted to keep it that way. Not only was it an embarrassment to her, but more than likely a death sentence to her brother who would ultimately kill the man who'd harmed her, and Riley couldn't abide that. It was also the reason she kept to herself, rarely letting anyone in, and stuck to the only world she knew of, the world she'd created when she emerged from her trauma. She clung to her books, reading them day and night, trying to find a world she could hide in, a fantasy that would swallow her up.

"Can I help you, Johnson? Maybe direct you to *your* office?"

"Got a smart mouth, don't you? Think you're all high and mighty. You'd be nothing without the Meredith Baker account, and you know it. You stole her away from me. She was supposed to be *mine*."

Dressed in an unexceptional black suit and blue tie, his brown mud-coloured hair was parted to the side and gelled, but he had a forgettable face with no distinguishing features. His sideburns were too long and his eyes were beady.

He despised her, especially because she managed the most profitable accounts.

"If you actually *did* your job, Johnson, she would've been yours, but you had me do the dirty work instead. Maybe next time you won't let manuscripts pile up on your desk and give some of them a chance for once. They might actually surprise you. There's a whole untapped market out there."

He thumped his fist on her desk so hard her pen bounced. "Watch yourself, Riley, because somebody might knock you off your pedestal and teach you a lesson."

She narrowed her eyes. "Are you threatening me? Because you can't push me around. Men like you make me sick, and unless you want to swallow your balls, I suggest you remove your useless hide from my office."

Johnson stalked towards the door, then sent her another glare. "One day, some man will get the better of you."

"Well, that man won't be you, Johnson. I'm not afraid of you."

"You should be." As he turned, he bumped into Megan, then blushed and apologised profusely. Riley rolled her eyes.

"You're Megan Bailey, right?"

She glanced between them before her gaze settled on Johnson again. "Yes. Do I know you?"

"Kenneth Johnson."

"Ah, Mr. Johnson." She gave Riley a wry smile and a look of understanding passed between them.

"I hear you're publishing again soon. Congratulations."

"Thank you."

"I'm currently accepting new clients. I can negotiate you a much better deal with the publishing house than you're getting with Riley. Being a senior executive has its advantages. You should consider making the switch. I could help you expand your profile, particularly your online presence and a larger portion of the overseas market. Your talent is being wasted in this office."

Riley gritted her teeth. *Self-entitled jerk.* She tried not to show her annoyance, but she was a Capricorn with an Irish temper.

She huffed in irritation as Megan smiled serenely.

"Thanks for the offer, but I like it where I am."

Johnson snorted. "You'll regret your decision. I

109

can make you so much more money."

"While I appreciate that, it is *my* decision and I've made the right one for me."

Johnson nodded, firmly put into his place. Megan was the loyal type and her protective instincts had flared.

She was immensely grateful to have Megan in her corner. She'd lost a few clients over the years because of money—another publishing house offering more for the contract—but never due to negligence on her part. She backed her authors and in return, she had their trust and friendship. Something men like Johnson couldn't understand.

He left, headed back to the hole he called an office. She was glad to see him go. He always put a damper on her usually high spirits.

***

"Wow. He seriously doesn't like you." Megan closed the door behind him.

Riley shrugged. "The feeling is mutual. How're you holding up? I'm so sorry I didn't stay. I know you needed me."

"I'm doing okay despite the circumstances, and don't beat yourself up. You're an amazing friend. Don't you ever forget that."

Riley moved from behind her desk. She was dressed in one of her expensive skirt suits, the colour a dark grey with a pearl silk blouse. Her red hair was in a neat French twist, and as usual, she had on a three-inch pair of heels, either Jimmy Choo or Christian Louboutin. Riley had done well for herself. At only twenty-eight, she had an impressive career under her belt and a wicked office with a prime view of the city.

But Megan sometimes sensed she wasn't completely happy, and while she enjoyed her success, she knew money and prestige had little sway over her editor. She'd seen her snap a heel or snag her expensive wardrobe with nary a curse or care. She wasn't even sure Riley knew of the labels she wore, only too happy to allow Michelle full control over that part of her life. Shopping seemed low on her list of interests and she was just as comfortable in jeans as this season's Stella McCarthy pant suit.

Riley seemed restless. Megan had mentioned it a couple of times, but she'd waved it off. She was very private, and Megan refused to push, figuring she'd talk if she wanted to.

"I just wish I could've been there for you. I don't want you to go through this alone."

Megan blushed. Riley raised an eyebrow. "Meg?"

"I wasn't alone last night. Detective Matthews stayed."

"Megan!" Riley's eyes lit up with scandalous glee and she offered an exaggerated wink.

"It's not how it sounds. He slept in Stacey's room." She didn't want Riley getting the wrong idea. Dean was only in her life because of Stacey, and he'd leave when she returned. Her heart sank. She'd come alive since he'd walked in her life, and she was afraid of who she'd become when he was no longer around. He did crazy things to her, things

111

she'd assumed were pure fantasy. Hell, she was a romance author, yet she was probably the most jaded of them all.

Still, Dean set her heart thumping. The morning could've taken a different turn if she'd let it. She felt like a shameless hussy. She should be thinking of Stacey, but instead her entire mind had been overrun by thoughts of hot, steamy sex. She needed a cold shower.

"I wouldn't blame you if you did something a little more than sleeping under the same roof. In case you haven't noticed, he's absolutely delicious."

She'd noticed, and then some, and it annoyed her that Riley had too.

"So that's how it is," Riley added. "Relax, Meg, he's all yours if you're game enough to go for him."

Megan blushed furiously. Her jealously must've been clear on her face. "I'm not sure that'll be appropriate."

Riley shrugged. "So? You could benefit from sex. Unwind a little and have fun doing it."

Megan rolled her eyes. "What about you, Riley? When was the last time you had sex?"

Riley's teasing smile faded. "We were discussing *your* potential sex life."

"That long, huh?"

She scowled. "I'm extremely selective. Besides, I've never met a man who made me feel like I could melt into a puddle on the floor just by standing close to him."

Megan understood that feeling. It was the way she felt around Dean. The man had far too much control over her body.

"One day you'll find that man, Riley."

She smiled softly. "I hope so. Someday." She turned back to her desk and slipped behind it, becoming the high powered executive she was.

Megan sank into one of the chairs designated for visitors, pulled out her laptop, and switched it on. She got comfortable, preparing to make the necessary rewrites on the sections of the manuscript Riley had made notes on and settled into her writing mode where she blocked out reality and merged completely within her fictional world.

The words flowed from her with ease and she shamelessly drew inspiration from Dean, incorporating him into Cole's character. No one would know but her. She liked knowing a piece of him would always be with her, or at least close to her. The novels she wrote were very real to her. She'd created them. She felt like they were a part of her, installing Dahlia with qualities she wished in herself.

She was interrupted when her phone rang and she was surprised that three hours had passed since she'd first sat down. She had almost finished the rewrites for Riley's approval and was happy with the results.

She glanced up as she answered her mobile to find Riley absorbed in whatever editorial task she was doing. Riley probably didn't even know she was still there. That was what made them such good friends. They had similar traits and could be extremely single minded on a project if they set their minds on it.

She took a sip of the iced tea that had been

placed on Riley's desk closest to her, and Megan figured Michelle had brought it in. The woman was exceptional at her job. If she'd thought Michelle could be persuaded, she would steal her away for her own personal assistant, but she was loyal to her boss. Riley had that effect on some people and she was certainly worthy of it.

She was definitely special.

"Hey, Don," she said into the mobile.

Amelia Donovan's brisk tone came through the speaker clearly. "You free for lunch?"

Megan's eyes widened. Amelia never initiated contact. It was always Megan harassing her until she caved. Dread filled her and she swallowed with difficulty.

"Sure. What's up? Is there news? Detective Matthews told me about who you think took Stacey."

She winced, hoping she hadn't gotten Dean into trouble.

"Unfortunately, there have been no developments. I just thought maybe you'd like to get something to eat and take your mind off things."

"You know me too well. I'll head over soon. I've just got a few more paragraphs to edit and then Riley's got to give me the okay."

"That's perfect."

She hung up, still a little surprised at Amelia for reaching out. Not that her friend was callous or selfish, she just wasn't much for offering comfort. She must think Megan was teetering over an emotional edge. Had Dean told her that he'd slept over? How she'd practically begged him not to leave her alone? If that didn't scream distraught and needy, she didn't know what did.

She was embarrassed, but it had taken everything to leave him that morning, and not climb into bed with him and forget, if only briefly, her world was crumbling around her.

She tucked her phone back into her jeans pocket and focused on her novel, but now her concentration was shot to hell as images of a naked and gorgeous Dean Matthews filled her head and her body warmed uncomfortably. Good heavens, she was acting like a cat in heat.

She should be mortified at her wayward thoughts, but she wasn't. It only made it clear she'd been allowing life to pass her by.

She felt guilty that she was lusting over Dean while Stacey was out there suffering at the hands of a homicidal killer who'd already sent five other girls to an early grave. She shivered as the images in her mind changed.

She refused to look up the Highway Dumper on the Internet. She didn't want to know about the man who'd taken her cousin and what he'd done to the other girls and would most likely do to Stacey. The graphic images in her mind were bad enough.

Chapter 18

Superintendent Amelia Donovan placed the fat file folder into her outbox to be filled by her assistant, Hallie Walker-Murphy. Her predecessor had a full-time assistant and she had inherited the wonderfully competent woman, but when she went on maternity leave, Amelia decided she didn't want any assistance, preferring to do the work herself. It wasn't until Hallie asked for a job to help pay for school that Amelia felt herself giving in to her adopted niece.

While Amelia loved her title job, it seemed like most of the time all she was doing was paperwork and dealing with bureaucratic bullshit. It wasn't exactly her forte, but she'd learned quickly how to get through the worst of it. Anyone had to be a damn fool to put pressure on her to make a decision, especially one that held lives in the balance. Which had been her main motivation for creating the taskforce. Each detective brought something to the table, having a mixed range of experiences and knowledge. As a collective, they were a powerful force. This was a maiden voyage, to see how the team worked a case together and how quickly a case could be solved by pooling intelligence and talents.

To say she was ambitious as hell would be an understatement, and fourteen years ago no one would've believed she'd become the superintendent of Harbour Bay's LAC.

Once Amelia joined the police force, she'd discovered that the discipline and opportunities available suited her. Her need to dominate served her well, helping her move up the ladder, off the beat, and into the detective's chair. Not long after that, she became the highest ranking detective in Harbour Bay and one of the highest ranking females in all of NSW. It hadn't come easy, but now she called the shots, and had the big office she used to type up reports and meet with her subordinates. Some of them relished the idea of a female superintendent, while others didn't. Growing up in Coleani's neighbourhood wasn't for nothing. She'd grown a thick skin, and there was always backlash, a reaction to every action, but she took it all in stride.

She liked to be a fair boss, but being boss also meant being a disciplinarian and it had taken weeks for her to read each file, determining which officers responded to praise and which ones required a steel-boot arse-kicking.

She stretched out her arms and back, her bones and muscles protesting. A twinge in her chest made her press her palm against the two-year-old wound. She took a deep breath and waited for the pain to pass. That was the problem with a scar; it was a constant reminder of a traumatic event. Not that she'd been awake for most of it, as the white-hot searing pain had sent her into shock. It hadn't been until she'd awoken in hospital that it became abundantly clear she'd been shot.

It had been more annoying than life threatening, and Amelia had been lucky that day, because the bullet missed her arteries. Long after it healed, the wound ached when she sat for too long without stretching. It was time to get up off her arse and go find real work. Her pants were tight, telling her to lay off the food and hit the gym.

Generally, she loved her job—making decisions that affected the outcome of cases, assigning them to the appropriate officers. But sitting for eight hours wasn't something she enjoyed.

She didn't like the politics that came with the position, either, and she'd already pissed off several people in her short stint as superintendent, but she'd caught the eye of the commissioner who believed she had a good brass set of balls on her and if she was after his job, she was certainly going about it the right way.

Crime in Harbour Bay had already gone down five percent in the last few months alone. She wasn't sure whether it was a reflection on her, or just a fluke. While Alec Harris had done his best in the position, he was of a different generation—one in which forensics had been a luxury, not a procedure.

Hallie peeked in the open door and smiled. "Hey, boss."

Amelia leaned back in her chair, a bone cracking

loudly reminding her that like everyone else she was human and wasn't immune from ageing, having celebrated her thirtieth birthday just a few months ago. "What are you doing here?"

Hallie, her face clean of make-up, her lips shining with clear lip gloss. She was dressed in a pair of black pants, a dark green square cut blouse and black two inch heels.

"Have you heard anything about Stacey Bailey yet?" Hallie asked.

She was about to reply when a knock sounded on the glass wall of her office beside the open door. She glanced over to see a young baby-faced officer standing there, his blue uniform clashing horribly with his ginger hair.

Amelia waved Constable Cade Watson into the office, watching him with narrowed eyes as he gave Hallie an appreciative glance. It was true Hallie had grown up, her amber doe eyes framed by the longest and darkest eyelashes Amelia had ever seen, and soft shiny hair pulled back into a ponytail, allowing the red brown curls to fall free down her back. Hallie had grown into her womanly curves with a tucked in waist and high breasts.

Cade stood before her desk looking much like a wayward child in a principal's office. His gaze remained fastened to his superior, rather than glancing around the room, almost as if using her as a lifeline. Many of the younger officers believed her to be a close cousin of the devil, and she didn't do anything to dispel the rumour. If you were an upstanding dedicated member of the team, you soon found Superintendent Donovan wasn't that bad and if you weren't dedicated, you'd learn the devil had nothing on Amelia Donovan.

She nodded to Hallie, who after grabbing the huge stack of folders from her outbox stationed on the desk, left the room, closing the door firmly behind her.

Amelia regarded Cade solemnly, knowing he'd had the highest grades in his class. He'd joined the Force at eighteen, straight out of high school, and had a list of recommendations and certificates a mile long. Like her, he was determined to be the best he could be.

His career goals cited a desire to supervise a team of his own, and he would; Amelia recognised herself in him. He would sacrifice a life with a family to get what he wanted, which wasn't necessarily a bad thing. The country always needed men and women who were married to their work, whose first responsibly and priority was to their job.

Some people were just dedicated to their country and providing a safe environment for future generations and sometimes that came at a cost—a high one.

"Constable Watson."

"Ma'am."

She indicated the chair on the opposite side of her desk and he sat down.

"Your supervisors are most impressed with your work, Watson, and have written many recommendations that have made it to my desk. I wanted to meet with you to tell you your actions are not going unnoticed."

Watson steadily held her gaze. She liked that.

She tended to intimidate many people. It told her he had a strong character, and she needed more men like Constable Cade Watson.

He nodded, accepting her praise. "I'm not going to deny that I want to advance, that one day I want to be sitting in the bull pen as a detective, but I don't do this job for the accolades," he told her.

She smiled. "I know. That's why you've come to my attention."

Chapter 19

Dean was having the worst time trying to concentrate. Despite his best intentions, his mind continued to wander to earlier that morning. After Megan had finally left the bedroom, he'd dressed—a task that had been quite difficult in his state of arousal—and found her in the kitchen. She'd moved about the space as if she'd been dancing, every movement graceful. She was dressed in jeans and a fitted tee, although he missed her pyjamas and would've enjoyed seeing her in them again—or out.

She'd caught his eye and sat him down on the stool situated beneath the overhang of her kitchen counter and had prepared him breakfast of eggs and bacon served with hot coffee. Then she'd sat down beside him and something within him shifted. Lightened. The scene had been so domestic. So comfortable. He'd liked it too much. The only thing missing was the perfunctory kiss on the lips before he left. But if his lips ever touched hers, it would not be a simple kiss. He would devour her, taste her, and explore her mouth until he knew her intimately.

Shit. He had to keep away from her. She was hell on his discipline.

She was attracted to him, for certain. Every now and again, he found her watching him, desire in her eyes. He knew he was the only thing holding them back. He almost laughed at the thought. Usually, it was the other way around. It didn't help that Megan was so attractive and sweet, smart yet funny—the perfect woman. Dean knew he couldn't possibly allow himself to get involved with her, but neither could he watch her get together with another man.

He let out a tortured breath. He seriously needed to get a handle on things. He glanced up and froze when he caught sight of her stepping out of the elevator some feet away. His heart sped up, leaving him breathless.

She gave him a wide smile as she approached and his body reacted. He was acting like a teenager just discovering girls. Hell, even when he'd been a teenager, he'd never had such a reaction.

"Relax. I'm not here to ambush you again."

"What are you doing here?"

She frowned at his abrupt question, her smile slipping. He wanted to kick himself. He was always saying the wrong thing around her and felt even more inept than usual. Yet, he hadn't done such a bad job last night. It was only this morning that he was messing up.

She held up an elegant boutique bag. "I've been shopping. I saw it in the shop window and thought of you immediately." To his surprise, she retrieved a milk chocolate brown shirt from the bag and handed it to him.

Dean glanced down at the shirt. It was the second time in his life a woman had given him a shirt. But knowing it came from her sent his whole body into a tailspin. "You shouldn't have."

"Relax. It wasn't my intention. I had to meet with Riley this morning for some last minute changes and the boutique is across the street from B&G. If you don't like it, that's fine. You don't have to lie to spare my feelings," she told him, obviously thinking of the story he'd told about the last woman. "Unless there's another reason for that look on your face? If you'd rather, I can get one for Nick too. Do you think he'd like a pink one?"

Dean chuckled. "You're something."

She smiled radiantly. "I hope that's a good thing."

"Very. Thank you. I like it and I'm not just saying that. So besides bringing me a shirt, what're you doing here?"

"I'm meeting Amelia for lunch. Apparently, she feels I'm about to board the crazy train, so she's requested my presence no doubt to gauge just how close I am to falling off the deep end. She probably has a point. I'm having trouble sleeping. My emotions are all over the place and I'm full of nerves."

"I have something for that."

"What?"

She studied him curiously. What he wouldn't give to know what was going through her head. Nothing he was bound to like, he was sure. Or maybe he'd like it too much, thinking of how he'd caught her staring at him when she thought he

124

couldn't see.

Was it his imagination, or had her voice taken on a breathless quality?

"Come with me."

Taking hold of her arm, he directed her to the elevator, jabbing the 'down' button.

"Where?"

"Just follow." Not that she had a choice with his hand keeping her captive. He hadn't meant it to sound like an order, his tone gruff with the level of control he exerted not to push this woman against the nearest surface and kiss her for all he was worth.

"Okay."

At first, he heard her reply as acceptance to the myriad of thoughts bouncing around his brain, but Dean quickly corrected himself and escorted her into the elevator. He seriously had to get a grip. She was the last woman he should be contemplating fooling around with, yet that didn't seem to stop himself from imagining all the ways he could take her. Breathing in jasmine and her subtle womanly scent, visions blasted through his mind and he fought to reveal nothing.

"How long is this going to take? I don't want to keep Amelia waiting."

"Relax. The boss is never ready when she says she'll be. Like most women," he added.

Megan's lips twitched. "You like her."

His gaze swept over her face, from her hairline down to her lips, then back up to those moss coloured eyes. He liked Megan better.

"She's fair and decent. Have a helluva lot of respect for her. Scrappy fighter. I've seen her take

125

down some scary blokes that even I didn't want to tangle with."

Amusement flicked over her face. "I don't believe you. I doubt there's anyone or anything that scares you."

You do…or rather, how I feel about you. Instead of speaking, he shrugged.

His skin burned where he touched her, his palm tightening in reflex. Forcing his hand to remain still, instead of stroking her like he wanted to, he stared at their reflections in the stainless steel of the elevator door. His lungs burned and he felt short of breath when he caught her gaze.

Not speaking or dropping eye contact, the air between them crackled with unseen energy, the tension building like the beginning of a brilliant storm, gathering in intensity. His mouth went dry, his stomach jittering with awareness and he felt the shift in her body where he continued to hold her and he knew without having to ask that she was feeling it too.

Chest rising and falling with quick breaths, Megan's lips parted, her tongue slipping out to wet them. He stiffened and her eyes widened as if realising what she'd just done.

"Dean." Her voice sounded more like a sigh, the single word drawn out long and soft. The doors to the elevator opened and relief spread through him. Any longer and he would've been pressing the emergency stop button. Rolling his shoulders, he stepped out with her by his side. She seemed perplexed when they arrived at the well-stocked gym filled with cardio equipment and weights. A large boxing ring filled the centre. She frowned. Clearly this wasn't what she'd expected.

It wasn't exactly what he wanted, either, not after the short elevator ride which had his blood pumping. He refused to acknowledge what had occurred just moments ago and where it appeared to be heading.

"Let's try working off some of those nerves," he suggested. "It'll do you some good. Besides, you could benefit from some self-defence lessons."

Not the brightest idea, considering how she'd made him feel in the elevator. Close proximity to her lush body was the last thing he needed, but he hadn't anticipated the lust filled ride when he'd planned this impromptu workout.

"Relax. I know how to do the single female thing."

Dean wasn't amused.

"I've seen you open doors. You need to be more cautious," he warned, an uneasy feeling settling in the pit of his stomach.

"I'll make a conscious effort to be more careful," she promised.

"Yes, you will. Stay here for a second." Without waiting for her to agree, he slipped into the changing area.

He swapped out his suit for a singlet shirt and shorts, his usual gym attire. When he emerged, he found Nick keeping Megan company. Jealousy raced through his blood, his muscles tensing. He forced his emotions under control, afraid he might take his partner's head off.

He stalked towards them, rubbing at the back of

127

his neck. Nick inclined his head in greeting and Megan's gaze followed his partner's, her eyes widening. An appreciative slow sweep of his body had him fighting back an inappropriate reaction; it would've been the second time he felt aroused in her presence within the last few minutes. She sucked her lower lip in between her teeth and Dean found himself mesmerised by the pulse frantically beating in her throat.

Nick chuckled.

Megan's face flushed, and Dean glared at Nick.

"You got nothing better to do?" he snapped, and his partner rocked back on his heels, thoroughly enjoying himself it seemed. *Bastard.*

"Plenty. I was just on my way back to my desk when I saw Megan," Nick replied. "You shouldn't leave her unattended."

His teeth gnashed together, the warning clear to him. Not that he believed Nick would go after her— what he'd meant was the other men in the building would pursue her. Beyond being an avid fan of her books, Nick wasn't interested. If Dean didn't have so much baggage, maybe he'd be the man for Megan. He couldn't, so he wouldn't start something knowing full well he would never be able to deliver. No matter how much they both wanted it.

"She's a grown woman, she can look after herself," Dean said.

Megan's gaze flicked between them, as if understanding there was something beneath their exchange.

"You're busy. I shouldn't have bothered you. I'll just go wait upstairs for Amelia." She took a step back, but he stopped her with a hand to her shoulder. "I'll feel better if you at least know the basics."

"Has anyone told you you're bossy?"

Nick snorted. "Understatement. You may as well relent, Megan. Dean's not known for giving up on something he wants. He'll relentlessly pursue until he acquires it."

For once, Nick appeared to be helping. Not that he wasn't grateful, but he'd rather they were alone. Still, an audience meant he had to be careful, which was better for everyone.

Megan's chest rose and fell with each quick breath. Something warred inside her, an emotion he couldn't name.

She muttered something suspiciously close to, "One can only hope" before sidling up beside him.

He took a deep breath, knowing he was about to get up close and personal with her, closer than in the elevator. This time, his hands would be on her body. He could do this, tangle with her in a non-sexual way. His heart thumped with anticipation.

"Have you ever taken a self-defence course before?"

"Once. I did some self-defence classes a couple of years ago as research for my book. I'm not exactly a physical person. I do yoga and the occasional walk to the shop for bread and milk, but that's about it. I really don't like to perspire."

She spoke in such a haughty tone that Dean laughed out loud. He bit off a groan as his mind teased him with images of teaching her to enjoy perspiring. It might take several attempts, but he was man enough to give it all he had. He shook his head, clearing it. He had to stop thinking that way. She was off-limits for many reasons, most of them his own. Still, that didn't stop him from giving her body one slow, long look that made her shift on her feet. He hadn't noticed how toned and strong she was from her yoga practice. Strange, since he knew exactly how many freckles were on her nose.

"Well, every woman should know how to protect herself." He climbed through the ropes into the ring and indicated his head for her to join him. "Come on, hop on in."

Her expression became one of unease, her gaze taking in the ring as a whole before narrowing in on just him. He couldn't be sure what was going on inside that pretty head of hers. Did she think he might hurt her? The thought left a sour taste in his mouth, his stomach knotting. He would never harm a woman. Never. But that didn't mean he'd never failed to protect one.

"If you'd rather another instructor, I'll be happy to teach you."

Dean glared at Nick. He hadn't been aware his partner was still there, his mind and everything else completely focused on this woman.

"Back off, Doyle," he growled.

"My, my…protective, aren't we? It was just a suggestion." Nick grinned, and Dean wanted to swipe it off his face permanently.

"Calm down, I'm coming. No need to bite anyone's head off." Megan climbed through the rope wall somewhat indelicately. Dean almost missed the sight because he'd been too busy shooting daggers at Nick.

"Okay," he began, "I'm not going to bother with the finer points. The only reason you'll resort to using these techniques is that you need to incapacitate a threat to you."

"With any luck, that'll never happen. They have to get close enough for me to touch before any of this will do any good," she said.

"I'll take the odds. Now make a fist."

He moved closer to Megan, shifting her body until she stood on an angle, telling her she made a smaller target this way. If she could move her body into a similar position, taking the time to correct the tiny fist she'd made, she'd be better off. Some people liked to tuck their thumb away, hiding it from view inside their fist like Megan did, but one good smack and that sucker was broken. Which is what he explained to her as he placed her thumb out of danger.

"Okay, the areas you want to aim for that cause the most pain are the insteps." He pointed to his feet. "Nose, solar plexuses and—"

"The family jewels. I know, women's rite of passage 101."

He glared at her, his hands on his hips. "And of course a man's most sensitive area. One touch and he'll be more worried about getting away from the ball crusher than for whatever purpose he pursued you in the first place. But just in case he's not discouraged, you'll need to know some other sensitive points."

Again, he pointed to his insteps, nose, and solar plexuses. "So, I'm going to attack you and you're going to fight me off. Most attackers will come at a women from behind, so turn around." He made a motion with his index finger.

***

Megan reluctantly turned, her gaze colliding with Nick's and he winked at her. Her heart thumped in her chest. She felt Dean come up behind her, grabbing her not so gently but not crushingly painful either. She didn't struggle against him. The heat of his body soaked into her and she melted against him.

Dean shook her, reminding her she was supposed to be fighting him. He leaned down and whispered the moves she was supposed to make. It took a long second before she reacted, her foot stamping down softly against his instep, pushing her body back into him as she jerked an elbow into his flesh before going for his nose. A quick hand blocked her punch at the last second before releasing, and again when she aimed her knee at his crotch. She had been wondering what he'd planned to do. Obviously, he wanted it to be as real as possible but the idea of hurting Dean kind of made the exercise fruitless.

He turned her body around before saying, "Again."

Had he been a drill sergeant in a previous life? Each time they ran through it, he demanded more from her, and each time she became faster and stronger until any would-be attacker would've been left wondering what had happened.

She jabbed him hard with her elbow wherever

she could reach him before sidestepping, going for his nose. He caught her fist before it made contact, then released it so she could continue with her counter-attack, her knee coming up slightly before he bowed his body, keeping his pride and joy out of firing range. Then Dean moved on to something even more difficult, determined to attack her every way he could, having her defend herself using the moves he'd taught her. She assumed he sensed how much fun she was having and wanted to drive the fact home that this was serious and not a game.

The fact he'd never hurt her defeated the point. He made sure he pulled his punches but all it did was arouse her senses, and knowing there were about twelve cops surrounding them was the only reason she didn't jump him. That scared her. She wasn't one to be ruled by her body, never wanting a man in such an animalistic way before. Not until she'd met him.

She was breathing heavily by the end of the session, her forehead slick with sweat, her face flushed. Her hands rested on her knees as she tried to catch her breath, her head almost between her legs. Megan hadn't believed she was unfit but quickly changed her mind as Dean ran circles around her. She gave him an unfriendly look.

"I think that'll be enough for today," he said, glancing at the clock on the wall of the gym.

"Good idea." She leaned against the ropes, no longer able to feel her legs.

Dean moved to stand beside her and she knew instinctively he was there to catch her should she fall. He probably thought her to be the most unfit person he'd ever met.

Meanwhile, she had to wipe her mouth to ensure she wasn't drooling. The man was completely gorgeous, his forest green undershirt clinging to his muscles. It wasn't fair for anyone to look that good.

She'd known sparring with the man could only lead to trouble. She already had enough trouble sleeping. She didn't need to recall in vivid detail the hardness of his body against her own. Their time in the elevator together was enough to fuel several dreams.

"You know, I started reading your first book."

Surprise had her eyes widening. She'd never expected him to follow up on Riley's suggestion.

He shrugged. "Granted, I haven't had much chance to read, but I'm far enough along to say you have a new fan."

She knew she shouldn't care what he thought. His opinion was one of thousands who read her book but she was thoroughly overjoyed that he'd liked her work. She wasn't sure what she'd do if he'd said it was mediocre or inaccurate.

"I'm glad."

"Nick even directed me to a few pages he thought I'd be interested in." The intimate smile had her stomach fluttering and her breath catching in her throat.

Her mouth hitched up. "I think I know the ones."

A flash of naked skin, twisted sheets and breathless pants raced through her mind, warming her blood. She shifted uncomfortably as a throb began between her thighs.

"You'd better get going. The boss won't wait

forever."

"I'll be more than happy to escort you," Nick suggested. He turned to Dean, adding, "You need to get changed."

She took a tentative breath. She could do with a shower, but unlike Dean, she didn't have a change of clothes with her. Hopefully, she could borrow something from Amelia. Her friend practically lived at the LAC. She was sure she had a whole wardrobe on hand somewhere in her office.

"Thank you," she said to Nick, looking at Dean to make sure he didn't mind. He seemed awfully protective of her—or possessive. She kind of liked it.

It seemed with each new meeting, the attraction between them grew. She'd never been so sexually charged to the point she believed she might be zapped from a mere touch. He felt it too, she was sure. The way he became taut in her presence, how he stared at her as though he wanted to devour her—it made her certain.

So, why did he hold back?

She wasn't comfortable making the first move, afraid of being rejected and embarrassed. She wasn't nearly as confident as the character in her book. Maybe he felt the same, which left them at a standstill. Could she be brave enough? Megan wasn't sure.

Dean didn't give her a chance to try. "Be careful."

His gruff voice made her stomach flip. If he'd meant it to intimidate, her body hadn't got the memo. "You too, Detective. I find I'm quite fond of you."

"What about Nick?" he asked softly, casting a glance over her shoulder at the waiting detective.

He was an attractive man, but when Dean was around, she didn't notice. Nick's hair was cut short, styled and parted to one side. His sapphire blue eyes laughed and his mouth, she noticed, was always quick to smile.

He was tall, almost on par with Dean. Guilt washed over her. She was constantly comparing the two men. Nick was a man of his own, and it wasn't fair to see him only as he stood beside the man she was lusting over.

"He's no Dean Matthews." She stepped through the ropes with even less coordination than when she'd entered. Her legs didn't appear to want to cooperate.

She felt the heat from his stare as she left the gym.

Chapter 20

The couple of days since Megan had left the boxing ring had been difficult. Dean had missed her terribly. He'd picked up his phone several times to make that small and tantalising connection but at the last minute repressed the urge to reach out.

He'd kept to his new promise of steering clear of her. Temptation was a dangerous lure and he needed to keep an emotional and professional distance. He hated it. His world seemed darker without her in it to provide sunshine, as stupid as that sounded. But it was true.

Megan lit up his life and made him feel things he hadn't in years—and for good reason. The loss of Tony and Emma had messed with him. He knew that. But that didn't mean he could easily move past it. Logic and emotion rarely went hand in hand.

He was finding it harder to concentrate now that he'd removed her from his life. He was constantly wondering what she was doing. Was she sitting alone in her apartment, teary-eyed? Was she even sleeping? He knew she'd had trouble in the past. He ran a hand over his head. He had to stop thinking about her and focus on the case. Unfortunately, he was no closer than he'd been when the killer first emerged. Fear clawed at him and Megan's heartbroken face flashed briefly in his mind. He should've never promised her a damn thing. He wasn't that guy.

But he wanted to be, for her. He wanted to be everything for Megan, all she'd ever need.

She'd overrun his life until he saw her everywhere—the gym, hell, even the taskforce's command centre. There was no freedom. He ached to see her. To touch her, to soothe her fears and comfort her. To give *himself* relief.

And he wanted to know how she felt. Was she going out of her mind too? He barely recognised himself anymore.

He was struggling to understand how he could feel so connected to another person in such a short time. His once cold heart was shattering, the tendrils of fear curling inside him like ice cold fists. Megan was seriously detrimental to his health and career and he was no closer to ignoring the effect she had on him.

Never before had a woman held his interest this long and it wasn't purely sexual, easily overcome by a night between hot silk sheets, although Dean admitted the image certainly had appeal.

It would be easy to take what he wanted, what his body needed. But Megan was unlike any other, and he wouldn't be any good for her. His heart refused to feel past the superficial.

He couldn't give her anything beyond the

moment.

His mobile began to ring, cutting into his erotic thoughts. He quickly removed it from his belt and answered the call.

"Another body has been found." Nick spoke the moment he answered, not bothering with pleasantries. "Murphy and Hill are already at the scene."

"They're certain it's one of ours?" His mood blackened. Another woman was dead. Another he hadn't saved. Her death was on his shoulders and his conscience weighed heavily.

"Absolutely. She was found off the King George Highway, just six kilometres west of the turnoff to Heavenly and has all the trademarks of the Highway Dumper."

Heavenly was the closest town to Harbour Bay. Small, the town's population hovered around a hundred and fifty and was policed by Gregory Fallon, a man who in Dean's opinion didn't deserve his position. He had wanted the case purely for its potential to be high profile, and the previous superintendent, Alec Harris, had pushed his weight around to get the remains of Carolyn Harper—the first victim—to the LAC after her body was discovered on the border between Harris's jurisdiction and Fallon's.

"Shit." He felt a moment of sheer terror and didn't ask the one question that was foremost in his mind.

He would know soon enough.

***

139

Dean stopped his dark blue Holden outside the temporary perimeter of yet another crime scene. The boys in blue had responded quickly, taping off the area with their blue and white chequered crime tape. Already the highway was becoming a circus, with several police vehicles providing a buffer between the scene and the highway. Many uniformed officers were directing the slow stream of traffic, hurrying along those who wanted to linger in hopes of getting a better look. Passengers held out their mobile phones and snapped pictures he was sure would be uploaded to their Facebook pages.

As much as Dean hated the public's morbid curiosity, he preferred them to the real vultures who'd already received a tip about the latest victim to fall prey to Harbour Bay's newest serial killer. Several news vans pulled up along the shoulder of the road, beside the marked police vehicles and their flashing blue and red lights.

Dean climbed out of the car, his hands going to his waist as he checked that his weapon and badge were easily accessible. He made his way to the uniformed officer assigned crowd control. The man looked too young, but Dean recognised the rookie constable as Cade Watson.

Cade nodded briefly as Dean approached, lifting up the tape for him to pass. He stopped in front of Cade, pushing a pair of Ray-Ban's into position, only too happy to delay the inevitable.

"You first on scene?"

Cade stood straighter. "Yes, sir. Call came in at four-twenty. I was over on Oak, my regular beat, and as the closest vehicle I responded immediately."

"What did you find?"

The man swallowed visibly and paled, his complexion making him look almost anaemic. The look didn't go well with the ginger hair.

"First dead body?" He hated it when cops taunted the rookies when they were sick over a body. Hell, they all went through it and it wasn't something a cop could forget. Dean still remembered his first body, not on the streets of Harbour Bay but on foreign soil, sand covering every inch of the land, blood splattered as far as the eye could see. He gave Cade some time, watching him regain his composure.

"Yes, sir. Never saw anything like that before. I guess you're used to it, though."

"Don't kid yourself, Watson. It doesn't get any easier and if it does you're in the wrong line of work."

Cade seemed to file that away somewhere inside his head. It was rare for the green officers to receive on-the-job wisdom from the men they looked up to.

"Yes, sir."

"Go on, Constable."

"So after making my way to the body and determining her to be deceased, I followed my tracks back to my vehicle and called it in."

"Good work, Watson, you'll go far in the job if you use your brains. Now, if you'll keep the vultures away while we work, I'd much appreciate it."

"Yes, sir." Another news van pulled up at the kerb.

141

Dean followed his gaze, noticing the *Harbour Bay Tribute* van. He frowned, his mood darkening as a parade of people scurried out, setting up their post beside the crime scene, the large heavy duty cameras clicking almost manically, shooting everything in sight, the vehicles, the road, the cars and him. He was sure he made a lovely subject, his hands on his hips, a frown on his face, feet braced apart, his weapon and badge showing since he wasn't wearing his concealing jacket.

His mood darkened even more when he recognised the slender woman in her mid-forties. Ava Barton was a career focused, anything for a good story ball-buster who was the bane of every Harbour Bay police officer's life. She was directing her staff, telling them what to shoot, where the best angles were and that she wanted the shots now. If Ava was here it was because she smelled a ripe story just waiting to be picked and twisted until it was more sensation than fact.

He turned away, giving the news reporters a shot of his back and ducked under the crime tape, taking the slight decline slowly before joining Nick, Matt, and Darryl at the base where the body of a decomposing woman had been discovered. Her body was bloated, her eyes pale and staring up unseeing. Dean hated looking at dead bodies when their eyes were open. It made them too human, made the death too real.

Matt quickly caught him up to speed. "A motorist wanted to take a shot of the scenery and got more than he bargained for. He wasn't expecting to see this, lost his lunch over by the tree."

Dean could understand why, and was feeling a little queasy himself. It wasn't the body that got to him but the length of time her body had been abandoned and rotting.

"Any idea how long she's been dead?" While the area had been canvassed after the past five bodies had been found, the King George Highway ran for several kilometres moving into two other jurisdictions and could've been overlooked. He made a note to check if the current dump site had been one of the areas officers had searched. It would help narrow down the timeframe of the victim's demise.

"I don't know, but while you were talking to Watson, I received a call from Stone telling me he was stuck in traffic."

"Can you believe it?" Darryl's hands went to his hips.

Dean's jaw tightened. "We should sell tickets to these investigations, we'd make a bloody fortune."

Nick's gaze narrowed on the news vans and reporters. "I see Barton is here."

"Yeah, expect to see yourselves in the paper tomorrow, gentlemen. Because I sense a shit-storm about to come down."

Matt crossed his arms over his wide chest and glared at the swarm of spectators desperate for a look at the morbid scene. Already reporters were standing before cameras and reciting a bunch of bull-shit to the avid listeners at home. Dean's stomach roiled as the closest reporter with wavy blonde hair and a tight shirt sensationalised the story she told her viewers, mentioning nobody was safe while the serial killer was still at large.

Dean listened as she told her audience she was live at the crime scene of the newest Highway Dumper victim and according to supposed sources within the LAC, the woman had been dead for a couple of days. To his disgust, the reporter speculated on what the police were doing, as if they were sitting on their arses.

Dean rubbed his hand over his clean shaven jaw. "Shit, Megan will be watching this."

"Go," Matt said. "We'll finish up here. Go reassure her. She'll probably be minutes away from a full-blown panic attack."

Dean nodded before jogging up the small hill and to his car, passing Doctor Stone and his assistant as they arrived on scene. His tyres squealed on the asphalt as he accelerated in a race to get to Megan, knowing she probably needed him.

He wasn't about to let her down this time.

Chapter 21

Dean banged his knuckles against the door to Megan's apartment thirty minutes later—a record in the afternoon rush hour. The door opened almost immediately and Megan stood there, clutching the door as if it was the only thing holding her upright. He hadn't bothered trying to call her, knowing what he had to say would be better said in person. Now he was glad of his decision, his heart pounding unsteadily at the beautiful sight of Megan Bailey dressed in simple jeans and a black fitted shirt. She was like a drug to him; the more he saw her, the more he wanted her.

"A body was found earlier."

"I know." Megan stepped aside, ushering him in. Dean moved inside and turned to face her as she closed the door behind him. "I wasn't going to panic. I was waiting for you to come tell me everything I'm imagining is just in my head, that I have nothing to fear." Her voice quivered and almost broke at the end as if she was about to burst into tears at any moment. She wrapped her arms around her body and looked up at him, her eyes wide as she chewed on her bottom lip.

"It wasn't Stacey. I promise you."

"Oh thank God," she murmured, appearing to relax.

"You need a drink." He stepped into her kitchen, grabbing the first two glasses he could find from a cabinet and opened the fridge to inspect its contents. No chick food, he was glad to see. He didn't mind the occasional salad or vegetable, as long as it was beside a large medium cooked steak. Megan followed him into the kitchen, bent down, and from the shelf on the door brought up what he was looking for—an open bottle of wine.

Dean poured the merlot into the two wine glasses Megan had retrieved from a cabinet, replacing his selections. He handed her a glass and took a deep sip from his. Megan did the same.

"Who was she?"

"We don't know, not yet. She was...it will be hard to make an identification..."

Megan fell silent.

He let out a deep breath and drank the rest of his wine, placing the glass on the counter with a large clunk. "Don't give up hope, Megan. Never give up hope. Stacey's out there. She's still out there." His words hung heavy in the silent room, uncertain who he was trying to reassure. But then he did something he never thought possible. He wrapped his arms around her and held her tight. Her body moulded into his, pressed hard against him, and he closed his eyes at the sensation, his body coming alive at the feeling.

"I know you'll find her, Dean. No matter what, you'll find her." She buried her head into his chest, her slender arms sliding around his waist and her fingertips grasping his shirt. Her warm breath seeped through the thin fabric, barely a barrier between them.

"Jesus, Megan, I don't know how long I'll be able to keep doing this." He stepped away from her, a fist tight around his heart.

Megan frowned at him. "Doing what?"

"Coming here, telling you to have hope when the cop inside me knows that one day I might be coming here to tell you Stacey's dead and then you'll cry and break my heart and hate me, and that'll be more than I could deal with."

Megan frowned, her eyes moist. "I won't hate you. I could never hate you. If Stacey died it wouldn't be your fault, Dean. Nor would it be mine. I might not like it, but I would rather it was you delivering the news." She moved away from him, back into the foyer and stood beneath the archway leading to the family room. "I'm not stupid, you know. I know you can't promise me anything, that Stacey's life isn't in your hands and that nothing you say will affect the outcome of the situation, but they're just words, Dean, words designed to comfort and that's all I need."

He muttered an expletive. *Real smooth, Matthews, way to ruin a perfect moment.* "I'm sorry, Megan. I shouldn't have said anything. I'll leave."

He barely got two steps when Megan spoke. "No, don't. Please stay. I need you here with me."

147

He turned around, his entire body taut with tension. His blood pounded in his ears as he absorbed her words, his gaze searching hers for sincerity. She was close to tears, her whole body quivering as if ready to give out on her completely. She *did* need him. He took a deep breath, preparing himself for what he knew would come next. Megan was too tempting for him to have any kind of choice.

He crossed the small space between them, and Megan's eyes widened at his speed. He caught hold of her head, cradling it on the perfect angle. Dean no longer wanted to fight it. He kissed her like he'd wanted to from the beginning, hard, rough, deep, a show of things to come. Megan's arms fastened around his neck, holding on tight as he continued to seduce her with his tongue.

The barely restrained passion and desire they'd kept bottled up ignited immediately and he heard Megan moan. It wasn't a mistake. Loving her could never be a mistake. Everything felt so right and never before had he wanted a woman more. His usual restraint was non-existent now that Megan was in his arms, almost as wanton as him.

It was pure comfort, he told himself, nothing more. He wasn't entirely sure who he was comforting, but at the present moment it didn't really matter. The only thought in his mind was Megan writhing beneath him in complete abandon.

He knew he should slow down, make sure this was what she wanted. He needed to know it was him she wanted, that not any man would do. But somewhere on the path from his brain to his mouth the words got lost along with any thoughts of slowing down.

He was going to break every rule, self-imposed and otherwise. He needed Megan. Maybe more than she needed him. She twisted him up, turned him inside out and nothing would stop him from having her. She was under his skin, buried deep, all the way to his soul. Usually, he'd be clawing his way out, but instead he found himself wanting more. Wanting everything Megan was willing to give.

Surprisingly, he didn't warn her like all the other women he'd slept with over the years about his lack of commitment. Didn't tell her she was making one of the biggest mistakes of her life by caring for him, letting him into her heart and body. He would never be able to reciprocate and he knew he would break her heart. But at that moment he simply didn't care. All he wanted right now was Megan. One hundred percent of her. How could he be so careless? That he could possibly destroy everything good in her? Who was he kidding? He wanted her, and damn his rules. He couldn't walk away, not now.

His hands slid from her face down the curves of her body to her waist, his rough calloused fingers working their way under the cotton material and onto skin so soft it was like touching silk.

Dean shivered in anticipation, the fabric catching between his thumbs and forefingers as he raised up her black shirt. His gaze zeroed in on the fact she was braless beneath and immediately after tossing the shirt away, his hands were on her breasts, revelling in the slight weight and perfection of them.

Megan's nails scraped against his stomach as she tried to rid him of his shirt. He allowed her a minute, raising his arms toward the ceiling so she could pull off the offending clothing. His hands felt empty and desolate without her filling them. Megan couldn't even wait that long and he heard his buttons pop as she parted his shirt, bouncing off the floor. Then her hands were on his chest, exploring, caressing with soft fingers.

Dean sought the zipper to her jeans and slid them down the flare of her hips and she stepped out of them, her underwear following. He lifted her into his arms and pressed her against the nearby wall, his hands grasping the backs of her thighs. Megan wrapped her legs around his waist. She kissed him harder and more desperately than before. He broke away to kiss a trail down her throat before shifting to take one beaded nipple into his mouth and sucked.

Megan's back bowed and she let out a gasp. He continued his assault, then moved onto the other. Her arms tightened around his neck and his nostrils flared at the scent of her. His restraint snapped. He released one thigh to stroke her, testing her readiness and found her welcoming heat, his finger slipping easily between her folds. Her body tightened around him, grasping at the finger.

He closed his eyes briefly, willing himself to get control, otherwise it was going to be over far too quickly. He added another finger, filling her, stretching her so that she could accommodate his penetration with ease. Her hips jerked as he increased the tempo and her breath came out in short, ragged bursts. He removed his fingers and Megan made a sound of protest that he silenced with a hot, wet, ravaging kiss. He wanted to be inside her when she came. He wanted that more than he wanted his next breath.

His moved his finger, slick with her passion, to his fly and after several frustrated attempts managed to shove his pants far enough down that his cock sprang free, hard and desperate for release. He shifted and angled himself at her opening, pushing the head inside. He suddenly froze. Swearing, he pulled away.

"Condom," he rasped, cursing himself at what he'd almost done. He'd never lost presence of mind, not until Megan.

"Where?" she asked, her voice husky, her gaze dark with desire. It gave him immense pleasure to know that he'd put that look on her face.

"Right back pocket."

Without another word, Megan's hand disappeared from his neck and in the next moment she had his wallet and was retrieving the condom he kept for emergencies. This certainly qualified. His wallet landed on the floor beside them. He let out a hoarse curse as Megan rolled the condom over his rigid length.

It took everything in him to keep from coming and when she started to pull away he stilled her with his hand, wrapping his and hers around the base of his penis, loving the feel of her touching him so intimately.

Megan squeezed gently and when he applied more pressure to her hand, she tightened until he felt a mixture of pleasure and pain. She ran her hand experimentally over him, watching his response before dropping down to his hardened flesh and positioning him once more at her entrance. She looped her hand around his neck as he pressed her into the wall. She exhaled deeply and her breath fanned over his heated skin.

He thrust into her with one long stroke before retreating and thrusting again, this time deeper, impaling her. Megan moaned his name and her head rolled back as he moved inside her, her body tightening painfully around his expanding flesh. His orgasm built. Every part of his body was experiencing pleasure, the slightest sensation almost too much to bear. His climax caught him by surprise and tore through him just as Megan's body tightened around him, milking him as she too found release.

When he was able to think again, Dean pushed away from the wall and started down the hallway to where he knew her bedroom was located. Megan made a sound low in her throat as his softening cock moved inside her with each of his steps. He deposited her on the bed and withdrew. She reached for him.

"I'll be right back," he promised and disappeared into the adjoining bathroom to dispose of the condom. When he returned, Megan was already beneath the sheets, her gaze steady on him as he removed his pants and shoes. Naked, he raised the sheets and slipped in beside her. He stretched out his body, feeling lethargic and at peace for the first time in years. Megan snuggled against him, resting her head on his shoulder as her hand settled on his chest. Her breasts pressed against him even as one of her legs moved between his own. She let out a contented sigh and her body relaxed as she drifted into a deep sleep.

Dean stroked his hand over her back, feeling the soft, naked skin beneath as he breathed in her scent and their lovemaking. Lovemaking? Sex, maybe. He'd never made love in his life, except that was exactly what he'd done and wanted to do again.

It should've terrified him. It would've, had it been anybody else, but Megan was different. He was different around her and when he wasn't with her, he wanted to be.

He wanted to possess her. Claim her as his own. In a way, she was his. He'd already given her a part of himself he'd never shared with another woman. He tried to block the rush of panic that threatened to swamp him. He was heading dangerously towards a place he feared and desired in equal measures. Sex was easy; it was the emotional side he couldn't handle.

Tony and Emma. He squeezed his eyes shut as their faces swirled in his mind. Not now. He didn't want to remember them when everything was so perfect. There would be time later to question, to blame. But for now he just wanted to enjoy this moment with Megan. It was beautiful.

His heart swelled as he stared down at her. In sleep, she looked younger than her years, vulnerable and innocent. He wanted to protect her from the world. He wanted to protect himself from the heartache he was setting himself up for. Already he hurt when she did, her pain a sharp blade to his gut.

It was more than he'd bargained for. He ached for her. Wanted her with a passion he'd not had in years. It was more than desire and it terrified him. It was the reason he kept his feelings out of his relationships.

The more he cared, the more it would kill him if anything happened to her.

Chapter 22

Dean woke up early as he always did. But this time was different. He was slightly out of sorts, his body oddly sated and rested. He was naked, but that wasn't anything new, because he often slept that way. He flexed his muscles, feeling the small stinging cuts on his back and the memory of the night before came back to him in a flood of ecstasy, boiling his blood and making him hard.

He turned slightly on perfume scented pillows— her pillow, her bed, and Megan sleeping soundly beside him, her body facing him. Dean's heart turned over just looking at her. She was so damn beautiful. Her porcelain skin ethereal, her long dark eyelashes resting against soft skin, her hand curled on the pillow.

The sheet that had once been around her chest, covering her breasts, was now down around her waist. She was baring herself to him, and he couldn't take his gaze away from her. He'd never been a breast man, preferring the whole package to just one perfect part, but Megan's body was the kind women would die for. He certainly would if he had his way...and what a way to go. He reached out to rub his thumb back and forth over one nipple, watching with fascination as it beaded. Megan moaned in her sleep, moving her body so that he had better access to them, opening herself up to him. The fire between his legs begin to smoulder.

He stoked her lovingly, from her neck down to her breasts and past her waist and hips, pushing the sheet further down until he could look at all of her. He hadn't had the time to do it earlier, his mind on other pleasurable things, but now he took his time, his hand moving over her flat stomach, a finger dipping into the small button hole of her belly and across her tucked in waist. Everywhere he touched was soft and warm and he couldn't believe how lucky he was to have tasted her, to have experienced all she had to offer and more. Even now he was having trouble believing it.

His hands cupped her mound, his thumb gliding along the parting lips of her womanhood, delving into the moist centre. Megan's head rolled from side to side on the pillow, her legs automatically opening wider to accommodate him, even though she wasn't yet awake. The thought of waking her was something he couldn't resist. He glanced quickly over at the clock sitting on the table beside her bed. He had a little time—not much, but more than enough. He didn't want Megan waking up to a cold bed. He opened the drawer beside him, having found a stash of condoms there. Once sheathed, he rolled onto her and entered her in one stroke.

Megan's arms encircled his neck, pulling him

closer, her eyes still closed. Neither of them could get enough. He withdrew and came back into her deeper and fuller than before, his hips grinding into hers as she wrapped her legs around his waist, riding the waves of sensations that came again and again. Her hips lifted and moved in unison with his, her body becoming tighter, the pressure building inside of her. She began to grip him harder, pulling at him. Her back arched, her breasts rising enticingly near his mouth and he took complete advantage, his teeth gently nipping at the hard buds before alternating between sucking and licking.

Megan writhed beneath him, close to climax. After the time they'd spent together last night, he'd learned all her signs. He knew what she liked, what got her there faster, what tortured her the most and had varied his technique. Megan convulsed, shuddering beneath him, and cried out his name. He surged into her once, twice more, and then followed her over into the sweet abyss.

Dean collapsed on top of her, catching his breath before gently removing himself from her and settled beside her, pulling her into his arms where she belonged. He'd made peace with that, though his brain still screamed at him for a number of reasons, all of which he'd tried to ignore. He was happy for now. Later he would properly dissect their time together, but for now he'd rather experience. Reality would always be there, but Megan would not. He was sure of that, despite her objections. One day, she will hate him. She didn't speak and neither did he. They simply rested, breathing into the companionable silence, her hand gently stroking his chest.

He kissed her silky hair, his arms tight around her, holding her prisoner against his hard body. They stayed that way for a while, the heat from his body sending Megan back into the world of sleep until he shifted and extradited himself from her grasp. She opened her eyes drowsily and looked up at him.

"I'm going to take a shower," he said.

She yawned, turning to look at her clock.

"I'll make coffee." She pushed the covers away but quickly covered herself, a blush rising from her neck as if he'd not touched and kissed every inch of her delectable body throughout the night.

Dean smiled as he stood, completely unperturbed by his nudity. "You don't have to do that. Stay in bed. Sleep. Unless you'd rather join me?"

Megan shook her head, looking at him over her shoulder. Her eyes widened when she saw his state of undress and tried very hard to keep her gaze on his face. She failed. Her gaze drifted over his form, lingering until his body began to respond to her blatant interest. She wet her lips and he groaned.

"As much as the offer has appeal. I'm needed at Riley's office in forty minutes and I'm sure you're due at work." Letting out a deep sigh, he sensed her regret. Stepping towards her, he grabbed her dressing gown off the back of a chair and handed it to her. She slipped it over her body, tying the ends together with a final tug. She sent him a smile, her face still sleepy, her cheeks rosy from their recent lovemaking.

He caught hold of the belt and pulled her towards

him, settling his mouth over hers. She sighed and leaned into his kiss, her arms stealing around his neck as she brought him closer. He took his time, slow and sweet, unhurried, enjoying the feel of her in his arms.

Her hands slid down his naked back, her fingers curling into his skin as the temperature rose between them. He broke the kiss and stared down at her, her lips wet. It made him insanely happy.

"I'm already late. A few more minutes won't matter."

Her hands stroked his chest, a satisfied look appearing on her face. "Hmm. What are you going to wear? I kind of ruined what you were wearing last night."

He remembered how wild and uninhibited she'd been. He'd seen a different side of Megan, one he knew not many men got to see. He grinned at her, pure appreciation in his eyes as he stared at her.

He tucked a strand of hair behind her ear. "Good thing it wasn't my new shirt then, wasn't it?"

Chapter 23

She would have to make a statement to the media, Amelia decided. The attack on the LAC from the press couldn't go ignored. It was times like these she wanted to be on the ground, actively pursuing the bastard, but all she could do now was remind the public that the police were doing everything in their power to put a stop to the horrible murders plaguing their city.

How had her predecessor Harris remained calm under the pressure? She wanted to educate them that real police investigations didn't work like on TV. No neat bow was tied after forty minutes.

But it didn't matter what she said. Nothing would change. The people were scared and her detectives hadn't caught the killer.

She would happily face the firing squad of the Harbour Bay media before allowing her men and women to be put under the harsh spotlight. They had a job to do and didn't need the exposure or harassment.

She knew they'd all be feeling guilty over the

newest body, especially Dean. He was the one she knew the least about, never offering up any information on himself, but she sensed a dark past that'd left scars on his soul. She had the power to look into his file, to ferret out his secrets, but she didn't. His past was his to bear, and if he wanted it to be known, that was up to him. She certainly wouldn't abuse her power.

She glanced over at the muted flat screen TV affixed to the wall inside her office. The news was running, and she recognised the crime scene flashed across the screen. She had to nip the police thrashing in the bud. It would only lead to further terror and a general bad feeling towards the people there to protect them. She couldn't afford to allow that in her town.

When she called Hallie into her office, her temporary assistant entered with her usual bounce. Her adoptive niece was always full of energy. She smiled, feeling lighter. Hallie seemed to soothe her without words whenever she was tightly strung.

"Set up a press release for later today."

Hallie nodded and went to work without another word.

Amelia leaned back in her chair thinking of Megan. She knew what it was like to feel helpless.

Their lunch the other day had been subdued. Megan was usually more vibrant. The strain she was under was obvious, and dark circles had marred the underside of her eyes, making it clear she wasn't getting much sleep. Amelia wanted to reach out, do more for her. But she was already buried in work and it wouldn't look good for her or the LAC to

161

appear to be showing favouritism. Because of her position, the last thing she could afford was to be emotional. It would undermine her job as superintendent and undo everything she'd worked for over the last few years.

Her hands were tied, so she'd have to rely on Dean or Nick to ensure her friend was looked after. Dean was a great detective, but not the least bit personal. On the other hand, Nick was a hard worker who got results. He could also charm the panties off a nun. Which made her wonder if she should allow him access to Megan. The last thing she wanted was for her friend to become emotionally entangled during this difficult time and wind up getting hurt. Nick was a bit of a playboy, at least according to rumour. Just how much of that was fact?

She let out a deep breath. She could hardly control every situation. It would be like trying to control the weather. She would have to wait and handle things as they happened.

Her head pounded as she stood, stretching and hearing her bones crack. She was getting old. Well, early thirties wasn't old but it was getting there. She certainly wasn't as spry and flexible as she had been despite her attempts in the gym to hold onto her youthful pursuits.

"Well, hello," a male voice said, his voice a deep timbre.

Amelia startled at the sudden intrusion into her space. Hallie stepped out from behind a tall man.

"Amelia, Prosecutor Carmichael from the DPP is here to see you," she announced.

The DPP was the Director for Public Prosecutions. Amelia nodded and Hallie disappeared quietly. She studied the man with the light brown hair, neatly combed to one side. He was dressed impeccably in a navy suit with a lilac tie.

"Aidan, please," he said. His gaze burned her as they swept slowly over her body. Her stomach flipped and she felt an answering heat.

She swallowed hard and smoothed imaginary wrinkles from her clothes, fighting against the need to fidget under his hazel gaze.

She'd heard of him from her friend Kellie, who worked upstairs, but she'd never met him. She'd been told he was a shark in the courtroom and won the majority of his cases.

He was also married, so she'd heard, but he wasn't wearing a wedding band. Not that she was remotely interested. He was much too polished for her liking. She liked her men rough and scruffy. She stared at Aidan's clean shaven jaw. She could even smell the subtle scent of his cologne.

"What can I do for you?"

"I've been assigned by the State to prosecute the Highway Dumper...when you arrest him, of course."

She raised an eyebrow and when she replied, her voice was cool. "So you've decided to come down here to push your weight around? I assure you my detectives are working extremely hard on the case. We want it closed just as much as your office does."

He smiled, showing straight, white teeth. "So protective. I wasn't doing anything of the sort. I just wanted to come down, introduce myself, and get some thoughts from you. I believe I've accomplished my goals although your estimation of my character is a lot to be desired."

She flushed. "I apologise. We're rather under the pump currently."

"I've seen the media reports. I take it you're not going to take the slamming lying down."

"No. I'm already working on a release."

"If I can assist in any way, please let me know." He handed her his card. "You can reach me anytime. Day or night."

She took the card and ignored what sounded like an invitation.

"I'm looking forward to working with you, Superintendent." He seemed to be waiting if she would offer a less formal title, but she wasn't about to. The idea of him addressing her by her given name was much too intimate. She felt she needed a barrier between them. She wasn't a fan of lawyers, even if he was on her side. And he was much too sexy.

Letting out a resigned breath, he offered his hand. She stared at it like she expected it to strike out at her. She was being foolish. She grasped his large hand in her smaller, softer one. His palm was rough with callouses that told her he was used to hard work and didn't spend his life in the office.

She shook it, making sure she exerted the right amount of pressure. It was all in the shake, she'd been told, and had spent time perfecting it. She'd worked for years in a man's world and was able to navigate it.

Respect shined in his eyes. She felt oddly

pleased, as if what this man thought of her had any bearing on how she viewed herself. *Crazy.*

"Carmichael."

Grinning, he leaned forward. "Donovan."

He turned and stalked out of her office. She stared after him. Kellie had never mentioned how sexy the Prosecutor was. But then, what did she expect? Kellie was blind to anyone who wasn't Darryl.

She shook her head. She needed to focus on the task at hand and not the overwhelming alpha male that was Aidan Carmichael.

Chapter 24

Megan tucked the corner of her sheet under the mattress, pulling it tight. The teal coloured Egyptian cotton matched the fresh doona that she had pulled from the linen closet. The hours had passed quickly from the time Dean had kissed her goodbye. She'd spent the morning taking care of mundane tasks to distract herself, but all she seemed able to accomplish was alternating between worrying about Stacey and daydreaming about Dean.

She'd never been one of those women who'd had booty calls or called a man home for lunch for a quickie, but Dean had seasoned her body into wanting him and wanting him *all* the time. Even changing her sheets hadn't helped rid her mind of a naked Dean lying in her bed.

She had showered, shaved, washed her hair, dried it, painted her toenails and moisturised all while on autopilot, her mind completely fixated on Dean. How he had felt against her, inside of her. What would she do about him? It wasn't as if they could have a proper functioning relationship. Every fibre of his body screamed at her, telling her he wasn't the one for her, but she refused to listen or obey. She would get what she could for now and worry about the rest later.

As she was putting her sheets into the washing machine, she heard a knock at the front door. Megan quickly added the powder and hit the start button, the machine automatically filling with water.

"Just a second," she called out, reaching for the doorknob before stopping short, remembering what Dean had told her about the peephole. Megan peered out and frowned, then opened the door to three women and a toddler

The one on the left spoke first, her brunette hair cut short, just dusting the tops of her shoulders. Her cobalt blue eyes sparkled. "Hi, I'm Natalie Murphy, and this is Kellie Munroe-Hill and Aimee Hawke. We're Dean's partners' wives." She motioned to the blonde beside her and the other woman, who had long chestnut hair. "I know this probably seems like a strange visit to you, but Amelia was concerned about you. Since she can't get away, she asked us to look in on you."

Megan felt confused and blamed it on the great sex she'd had last night and this morning. She stared at them before catching sight of the large belly of the woman in the middle.

"Oh my God, you're pregnant. Please, come in. I am so sorry. I'm not usually like this. If you're friends of Amelia's, you're certainly friends of mine." She gave them the best smile she could and directed them into her family room. The blonde with the large protruding stomach, Kellie, collapsed on the couch as she rubbed her swollen belly. Natalie sat beside her and the toddler crawled into her lap.

"Let me make a pot of coffee." She looked forward to a few moments of peace to reflect and regroup.

"No, you sit down, I'll do it." Aimee placed a hand on her shoulder and squeezed. "That's what we're here for, to help make your life easier."

She went to the kitchen, and Megan noticed she had no trouble finding what she needed. She sat down in her recliner somewhat tentatively, eying her guests. She wasn't good with people, especially new people.

She dealt much better with fiction than reality. In her books, she could control everything, say what she wanted when she wanted to, and only when she decided. She'd never liked the unknown factor and had made a safe environment for herself, except that safety was only just another figment of her imagination. Nothing was ever truly safe, and no one could ever really be prepared.

Unsure of what to stay or what to do, she asked Kellie, "How far along are you?"

She smiled proudly. "Almost nine months, and about time, too. I feel like I'm going to pop if I get any bigger."

Megan agreed silently. Her apartment wasn't the place for a woman to go into labour. She wouldn't know what to do, and childbirth was bad enough with a bumbling buffoon nearby.

"Do you know what you're having?"

"No. My husband, Darryl, and I want to be surprised."

Megan nodded and fell back into silence. Soon, Aimee brought mugs of coffee into the living room.

"How are you doing, Megan?" Natalie's concerned gaze washed over her.

"About as can be expected." She clutched her coffee mug, gaining solace from the heat. "It's a nightmare I haven't woken up from."

Aimee squeezed her knee. "Last night must've been a scare. How is Dean working out?"

Megan burned her tongue as she swallowed the coffee. Her face heated, and she hoped it didn't announce to everyone what she'd done last night.

"Fine," she said, her voice quavering.

"Dean can be…he doesn't do well with emotional women. I hope you don't judge him too harshly."

"He's under a terrible strain," Natalie added. "Sometimes he can be abrupt."

Were they talking about the same man? She squirmed in her chair, feeling awkward.

"Dean's been great," she said. "Comforting."

"Nick was right." Kellie watched her closely.

Megan wondered what the hell that meant as her heart raced and her stomach flipped.

Had Nick mentioned something about them? She didn't want Dean to get in trouble. Unless he'd revealed that he'd spent the night in her bed? She trusted him not to share something so intimate with anyone, not even his teammates. Not that she was ashamed or embarrassed, she just didn't want her personal details broadcasted.

169

Though, Nick needn't know what happened last night to make an assumption about them. He'd witnessed them together, seemed to find them amusing. If they'd guessed at their relationship, it was her own fault.

The women shared surreptitious glances. She didn't like it and wanted to know what the hell it meant. The toddler slid from her mother's lap, wandering around on wobbly legs. She was so small and cute that her heart ached.

Don't even go there, she warned herself.

"I'm sorry I don't have any toys for her to play with."

Natalie waved her hand. "That's okay. Maddie can find just about anything to play with." She watched her move towards the gleaming Stratocaster in the corner. "Don't you dare, Madeline Jane." While the motherly reprimand had Megan sitting straighter, the toddler didn't seem unnerved and offered an innocent looking toothy smile. "I'm so glad another baby is on the way," Natalie added. "Someone closer to Maddie in age. I was beginning to worry."

Kellie laughed. "Natalie's a psychologist. Can't you tell?" Her tone held affection.

"Yes, I am. Can you tell that Kellie is a police sergeant, complete with the mocking insincerity of my profession?"

Megan smiled. It was clear these two had played this game before. Settling back against the cushion, she listened to the women as they bantered. Aimee had been quiet, but maybe that was her personality. She smiled indulgently at her friends and winked when she caught Megan's gaze. They talked for a long while. Maybe it was good that Amelia had sent them over to check on her. She didn't have many friends, and couldn't remember the last time she'd had people over. It felt good. It eased her loneliness, and that was enough.

Chapter 25

Leaning back in his chair at the LAC, Dean wanted nothing more than to be in the gym several levels below. His hands itched for the feel of the black plastic of a boxing bag. But right now he didn't have time. He didn't even think he had the energy. Last night's activities had depleted him. Despite how good it made him feel, he was still asking himself what the fuck he'd done.

He shouldn't have touched her. Shouldn't have gone to her apartment. Shouldn't have comforted her. But he had been powerless at the time, unable to think, the burning desire for her overruling any sane and rational reasoning he had. Even now he could feel her smooth silky skin beneath his fingers. He recalled how she'd quivered and contracted beneath him and he cursed silently as his body began to respond.

What the fuck had he done? He'd just complicated an already complex situation. Amelia was sure to skin his hide when she found out. Not that he was afraid of her. Megan was a consenting adult and they'd done nothing she hadn't wanted. Just the memory of taking her against the wall had him hardening painfully. A state he was getting used to around her.

Still, he wasn't a relationship type of guy. He hadn't hidden that fact, but he'd wanted Megan to the point of insanity and had taken her. He didn't try to lay the blame elsewhere. He'd known what he'd been doing the entire time and it hadn't stopped him. If he was honest with himself, he would repeat it as often as possible given half the chance.

He should never have touched her, but what was done was done and he didn't regret it. However, Megan could get hurt and that was the very last thing he wanted.

He ran a hand over his face. Last night had been the most erotic experience of his life and he'd never come as hard, never been so ready for more after the first time with her.

She was like a drug, and no matter how many times he had her, he still wanted more. He was insatiable.

He wished he could pretend indifference. He was tired of fighting. What was he to do? He couldn't back down now even if he wanted to. He'd play this to the bitter end and he was sure that was exactly what it would be. Bitter and the end of something wonderful.

Then Amelia would kick his arse and make his life miserable—at least more than it already was. As if just thinking about her conjured her, she appeared in the command centre.

"How's it going?"

She was dressed in a sunflower yellow blouse that complemented her mocha skin. Her black skirt accentuated her hips and narrow waist, her body toned and muscular. She was a larger woman—not fat, but strong—and she could put a man three times her weight on the floor in a matter of minutes. He'd seen it done.

Her dark hair was pulled into an elegant twist on the back of her head, her cheekbones more prominent and her dark eyes highlighted by understated makeup.

Since taking the role of superintendent, she'd slowly morphed into a more professionally coiffed woman. Not that he wasn't absolutely sure she could still get down to her violent roots and flatten a man.

"Frustratingly slow. For all we have, we've got fucking nothing," he told her.

He was tired of being several steps behind the bastard. He wanted to catch him, not just for Megan and Stacey but for every one of his victims and their families. Amelia squeezed his shoulder gently.

"You need anything?" Instead of demanding he close the case, she was on his side—a cop first—and he was grateful for her support.

"A lead. Just one."

"I might be able to help with that." As he stepped into the command centre, Nick popped a Tic Tac into his mouth.

"How long has she been missing?" Dean asked.

"No one knows. Her relatives thought she'd just taken off. Apparently, it wouldn't have been the first time. She's been dead only a couple of days."

"We were lucky to find her when we did."

"Real lucky, because Doctor Stone found something more," Nick said. "Something small inside the bloodstream."

Dean sat up straighter, intrigued. "What?"

"A dose of Sodium Nitroprusside mixed with household ammonia and bleach, but he said it wasn't ingested."

"Sodium Nitroprusside?"

"SNP. Stone says it's used in cases of hypertension, to lower the blood pressure, and although it's taken intravenously the Doc couldn't locate an entry point."

"So that's how he's killing them." It wasn't a question. He'd always wondered, and knowing they'd starved to death hadn't sat right with him. "I take it the SNP isn't widely available?"

"No. I'm checking with medical supply sellers, hospitals, pharmacies, even vets, and so far none are missing any stock. Private buyers all have legitimate reasons for their purchases and have been vetted. I'd say he's using an old stash."

"Expired drugs can either be ineffective or extremely dangerous."

He glanced over when the door to the elevator opened and Darryl, along with Matt and James, disembarked, their hair still wet from the shower. He frowned and rubbed the back of his neck.

"Hey, if you told me you were hitting the gym, I would've joined. I could use a good fight," he said as they approached.

"Next time," Matt said. "You and me in the

175

ring."

"You got yourself a date, Murphy."

Darryl opened his desk drawer and withdrew his weapon holster, clipping it to his belt. Dean noticed James and Matt do the same. Darryl caught his gaze. "Dinner at Tanner's. We all need the break. You in?"

Normally he would've said yes, but all he could think about right now was Megan and getting back to her. It had been almost eight hours since he'd last seen her, heard her voice. He shook his head. "Nah, next time."

James frowned. "You're not going to stay here all night, are you? You may be good but you need a break just as bad as we do, if not more. This case is getting to you. We can all see it."

Dean raised an eyebrow as he looked at the members of the team. Of all of them he was the most closed off. In fact, his co-workers didn't really know him, knew nothing about his past. It was an unspoken rule that he did what he wanted and that was it. For James to say something about his attitude had him at a disadvantage. They didn't usually analyse one another; they preferred to leave that up to Natalie, who absolutely loved the task.

"You'll burn out if you keep this up," James said. "I know you want to find this guy. We all do. Don't forget that. I know you have a personal stake in this. Nick mentioned your promise. I get it. We all do. But step away, Dean. At least for tonight. If you're not up for company, then go home. Get some sleep, whatever, but you need a night off."

They were right. Despite the break in the case, he

knew the results of Nick's search would not happen overnight and staying would only lead to frustration.

He held up his hands. "Relax, I'm not going to be working. I just have someplace I've got to be."

James nodded. "Well, you know where we'll be if you change your mind. What about you, boss?"

"I've a couple things left to do before I can clock out, but yeah, count me in. The thought of Tanner's is making my mouth water. Don't stay too long," she told Dean before following James and Matt out.

He was going to enjoy his night, too—in the hands of a loving woman. He stood, collected his things and made his way to the parking lot. The need to see Megan, to hold her in his arms, was strong. As much as his subconscious told him to stay away, a pull existed between them and he could no more deny it than he could deny breathing. He didn't know what this was, but he knew he wanted to be in her company and would remain there until he'd seen this through.

Chapter 26

As he knocked on Megan's door, Dean's body tensed. He had to see her, touch her. His need for her almost frightened him and hadn't subsided since he'd left the LAC. It had doubled and grown in magnitude and intensity. He could almost smell her perfume or maybe that was just leftover residue from the night before. God, how he wanted to sink himself into her. He'd never wanted anyone so much. Everything about her set his blood on fire. The anticipation of her welcoming arms and body surged through him. He waited, slightly impatient, for Megan to answer. It wasn't long, but the way Dean was feeling, at how much he wanted to join them together, how much he needed to kiss her...it was torturous.

She opened the door, only slightly, and smiled at him.

She looked good. Her mahogany hair was loose about her shoulders and her feet were bare. The dark blue jeans were tight, showing of her shapely thighs. She was wearing a white shirt with the Pink

Ribbon logo on it. Her face was clean of make-up like usual and after last night he knew the exact number of freckles of her nose, having counted them all while lying above her.

"Hello, Detective Matthews."

Dean raised an eyebrow at her formality, especially after all they'd shared. He was about to comment on it when she opened the door wider and his gaze fell on the three women in her kitchen. Ah, that explained it. He hoped. He hadn't even considered she might regret their time together.

He stepped past the threshold, his stomach knotting.

"Ms. Bailey, how are you?" He nodded to the women. "Ladies."

"Detective," Aimee said from her perch on the kitchen stool beside Kellie.

"Dean," Natalie and Kellie both said, slightly on a more informal basis, having spent longer getting to know the little bit he dared show.

"What're you doing here?" Natalie asked, and he held her curious stare.

"Just checking on Ms. Bailey. It's a stressful time. I wanted to see if I could help in any way."

Megan's eyes sparkled in obvious memory of the way he'd *helped* her. The knot in his stomach eased a little. She didn't appear to be regretting last night.

He addressed the women. "What are *you* doing here?"

"Same reason," Natalie replied. "Amelia asked us to check in, thought we'd be able to keep her company, see if she needed anything."

That explained it. Dean knew it was rather

unorthodox for them to show up, but Megan's close relationship with Amelia was the only excuse they needed.

There was a squeal before a little girl ran toward him—a miniature version of her mother—from around the kitchen counter where she'd been hiding, her face covered in vegemite. Her brunette hair was pulled into pigtails held by a pink ribbon. She latched onto his calf and clung to him.

She would be a handful, as evidenced by her eyes sparkling with mischief. She had everyone around her—himself included—wrapped around her little finger. Maddie was a sweetheart, and made everyone want to spoil her. But she was also intelligent, and anyone coming up against her in the future would find themselves losing the battle.

She had so much energy. If he ever had children, would he or she have the same strong personality as this little girl? Jesus, he realised he was imagining a little girl with mahogany hair and green eyes.

"Dean," Maddie gurgled, her arms tightening around his leg.

Rubbing his hands over his face, he felt the prickly whiskers on his chin. "Come on, Maddie, you're ruining my reputation."

She latched onto his hand and yanked it closer to where Megan stood. "Meet Aunty Megan." Megan's name came out more like *M'can*.

Dean raised an eyebrow at the title she'd already bestowed on Megan. *Aunt* sounded so right.

"Come on, Maddie, time to go. Now, don't frown at me, young lady," Natalie said sternly.

Dean caught Kellie's eye as he stood beside

Megan, his body half protecting her from what dangers might lurk near her. He gave Kellie a look that dared her to comment, but she just smiled and winked at him as she rubbed her belly. He scowled.

"Let's get a move on, I need to sit down."

Aimee frowned. "You just stood up."

"You try standing for two."

Aimee turned to Megan. "Thank you for having us here today. I hope to see you soon. In fact, we're just about to go to dinner. Won't you join us? Dean, what about you?"

"We're staying in." He spoke before thinking, his desire to be alone with her making his tone sharp. He wanted to be here with her, but he hadn't meant to say it out loud.

Megan froze beside him, her eyes widening and he realised how he'd sounded and what his words revealed.

There was no use keeping it a secret. Especially with the way she kept looking at him. Did he want to keep it quiet? There was no conflict of interest, nothing but the knowledge that one day it would end. This wasn't the beginning of something special, only raw passion in a troubling time.

He could see Natalie's fascination. What was going on in that shrink brain of hers? She no doubt knew exactly what was going through his mind. Her gaze moved from him to Megan and back again, a warm smile curving her lips in satisfaction.

"Actually, I'd love to go out," Megan said.

Dean held her gaze, trying to gauge if she was okay with his announcement. Perhaps she wanted their time together to be kept quiet? When he saw no reprimand on her face or censure in her eyes, he assumed she was okay. Good, because he was nowhere near done with her.

Moving forward—in more ways than one—he took Megan's arm, noting the sparkle of pleasure in her jade eyes. "Out it is, then."

Chapter 27

Twenty minutes later, Dean parallel parked in front of Tanner's. He'd been quiet the entire trip. He was no longer sure he wanted to show off Megan and his attraction to her. He didn't like the idea of sharing her, even with a bunch of married men who wouldn't even think about Megan as anything but a victim's cousin and whatever the hell she was to him.

Megan climbed out of his car, her whole body practically alive with excitement and anticipation which was the only reason he didn't stuff her back in the car and return to her place. She glanced about the parking lot, her gaze fixating on the small seventies era building that was Tanner's. It wasn't five star but it was the only place you could get a quality steak on a budget.

Her expression hadn't changed. He admitted to himself he'd half expected to see her petite nose scrunched up in disgust. Money was one of the many differences between them. But he reminded himself she hadn't always been wealthy. She'd grown up on the road, touring the country with her roadie mother and musician father. This wasn't the first place she'd been in that resembled a dive.

Her green eyes sparkled, warming his heart. She seemed at ease and he tried to think of a time he'd ever seen Megan glammed up. He doubted she was anything other than what she represented.

Up ahead, he could see Matt, obviously having gone straight from the LAC to the bar for a few drinks and a round of pool before his wife arrived. The two greeted each other before Matt kissed his daughter on the cheek. Matt's gaze meet Dean's and he nodded, trying and failing not to look so interested in the woman walking beside Dean.

He sighed loudly. Damn he should've known this wasn't going to be easy. He was going to have to put up with their sideways stares and speculation, not to mention the crap he was sure to get tomorrow. Luckily for him he had the late shift with James who still wasn't quite sure about Dean and wouldn't rib him too much out of not knowing if Dean would reciprocate—and painfully.

He sensed Megan watching him and he glanced down at her, offering her up a smile as they reached the entrance of the building. He opened the door and waited until she preceded him. Immediately coming face to face with James who had a beer in one hand and the other on his wife's hip.

"Glad you could make it, now the teams all here," James said ignoring the elephant in the room. "We've got the table in the back, eleven. I've already requested two more place settings."

"Thanks, James meet Megan Bailey, Megan,

Detective James Hawke."

"Nice to meet you." She shook his hand politely. He seemed reluctant to remove his grasp from his wife's hip, and his hand returned there immediately after the greeting.

Had Megan noticed the curious glances aimed her way? What must she think? She was bound to have questions and he wasn't sure he wanted to answer them. This was why he hated relationships. He wasn't a talker and he never spoke about his feelings—or his past.

She leaned into him, either to reassure him, sensing his inner turmoil or for courage herself. He probably wasn't the only one feeling out of sorts. Neither he nor Megan were very social people.

This night was for the both of them. They both needed the night off from worry and fear that Stacey may never be coming home. Every time his phone rang he was tense with fear that it was someone informing him that another body had been discovered.

"You too. Want anything to drink? I'm about to order."

Dean ordered for himself and waited until Megan decided what she wanted which was a lot like pulling teeth. The woman couldn't make up her mind. Of course it didn't help when she was interrupted half way through when Amelia arrived. Megan swooped in to give her friend a hug and to everyone's surprise it was returned. He didn't miss the look he got when it was explained to his boss that Megan was here *with* him.

It was almost humorous. Part surprise, part death

glare. He would definitely be hearing about it later.

"Come on, let's sit down." He steered Megan away down the narrow aisles, nodding towards Tanner who was manning the grill on his way. He found the horseshoe shaped booth immediately not just because he often dined at Tanner's but for the group surrounding it. Matt was busying attaching Maddie into the booster seat to notice them arrive but he did catch Darryl's startled look which he quickly hid and began to fuss over his wife, seating her beside him at the table.

Tanner's was a low rent establishment with wood tables and booths complete with ring stains from glasses and beer bottles, the word coaster alien to the owner. The floors were also wood and the soles of your shoes often stuck to it. The bar was stocked with four different types of beer, a house wine and of course the great men, Jim, Johnny, Jack and not much else. The place could be described as a dive, but had great atmosphere. A couple of big screen TV's were mounted above the bar playing the most recent sporting event. It was also one of Harbour Bay's best kept secrets and wasn't for everyone. Tanner's didn't sell salads, just steak and any other dead animal that could fit on a grill and other than nacho's the only thing on the menu served about twenty different ways.

Dean introduced Megan to Darryl and when Matt had finished with Maddie, him also. They were all polite, casting him a few looks when they didn't think he was looking but thankfully didn't say a word.

Nick appeared beside Amelia. He too had a beer

in his hand and what appeared to be a phone number scrawled in black biro on his hand. Dean pulled Megan towards him and away from Nick, earning him a glare from Megan as he boxed her in between himself and Maddie.

Within ten minutes they were all sitting in their seats, drinks before them as they awaited their meals. Matt raised his glass in a toast and they all followed suit. "To good friends and amazing wives. May no talk of work pass our lips tonight."

Natalie raised an eyebrow. "Poetic."

Matt shrugged as they all clinked their glasses together and talked of sports—who had the most chance of winning this year—and regaled everyone with funny stories and memories. Natalie and Matt gushed over tales about Maddie and Hallie, while Kellie complained about how swollen she was, saying she was the size of a house. All the men immediately told her it wasn't so. By the time the food had arrived, not one word had been uttered about work or the case.

Chewing on a piece of steak, Dean savoured the taste. It was the only time he ever ate like a king, often opting for take-away or microwave meals when he was at home. He didn't mind cooking, having learned the basics in the army, but the effort was wasted on just himself. He glanced over at Megan who was biting into her burger, tomato sauce dripped down the side of her hand, and if they'd been alone Dean would have licked it off her. She must have sensed his fascination, because a second later her tongue was lapping at the sauce, a warning look on her face.

187

He smiled and took a sip from his own beer. The conversation had moved around to this afternoon and Natalie was talking about how Maddie had used Megan's many books as blocks, building herself a little city. Kellie added her own comments and earned a glare from her husband.

"You should be resting," Darryl scolded his wife. "The doctor told you to take it easy as you finish up your term."

Kellie rolled her eyes. "I'm pregnant, Darryl, not dead. But you will be if you don't quit it. Besides, that *advice* was given by a coroner not a GP."

Megan's eyes widened and her mouth dropped open. A piece of beetroot slipped out. Dean reached over and stole the slice of beetroot from her plate. She batted away his hand.

"So Megan, spill it…we're all curious," Darryl started, ignoring his wife and Dean's shocked look.

Was he about to be publicly humiliated? He could deal with it, had endured it at school for the better part of his primary school years, but it wasn't a nice feeling and he'd hoped not to drag Megan into it. Shit, they hadn't had time to talk much to each other about anything besides the case. She had no idea this was the first his team had seen him so attentive over a woman or with a woman at all. He needn't have worried, though, because that was not what Darryl wanted to know.

"How is it you and the boss became friends?"

Dean glanced at Nick, who'd obviously not told them his part in the friendship.

"Well, a couple of years ago I called the LAC and asked to be put through to a detective so that I could ask some questions. I wanted to make sure my novel was as accurate as possible," she explained. "So I was told they'd connect me with someone and the next second I was on the line with Don and she agreed to read my novel and let me know everything that was wrong with it."

Matt grinned. "That sounds like Donovan. So how much red did she put on the paper?"

"Hardly any," Amelia said. "The book was well written and researched. There were just a few inconsistencies but they were ironed out."

"And a beautiful friendship was made?" Nick smirked.

"You didn't tell them your part in this?" Dean grinned when Nick's face went blank.

Amelia took a sip of beer. "Your part?"

"The call originally came to me," Nick admitted, "but I thought it would be funnier if you took it."

"You're a real shit, you know that, Doyle? Seriously, how do you put up with him?" She addressed Dean.

"He has his uses," Darryl said.

"Oh, well. It all worked out in the end and I count Don as one of my closest friends. However, I would like the opportunity to add you all to that list."

"Don—as in Donovan? Cute," Nick said. "We all know the boss isn't one for nicknames."

Amelia scoffed. "But I'm sure I have plenty behind my back."

"No one would use those around us, boss, if they want to keep their heads," Dean said loyally.

Amelia replied with a nod of gratitude.

"Actually, it was funny it worked out that way but I was thinking more along the lines of Don Corleone, as in the boss. I thought it fitting."

There was a moment in which everyone absorbed that.

"Eat your vegetables, Maddie," Natalie told her daughter.

The little girl picked at her broccoli, placing it beside her mouth before dropping it over the side of her booster seat. It bounced off the small gutter of the chair and landed in Megan's lap. She glanced over to see the sleight of hand as Maddie continued to lift her vegetables to her mouth before pitching them under the small table attached and releasing them to the floor. Megan grabbed hold of the second broccoli stalk before it hit the ground, adding it the first piece sitting on her napkin resting on her lap. Moving slowly, to avoid detection, Megan caught hold of Maddie's hand, relieving it of the vegetable about to meet a horrible death and placed with the others. Dean smiled at the cheeky action. Partners in crime. He should've known Megan would aid rather than report.

He placed his hand on her thigh and squeezed lightly. She didn't show any outward signs that she felt him, but then her hand came and rested on his. At first he thought she was about to move it off her and to his surprise his heart seemed to stop, his blood running cold, but all she did was wrap her hand gently around his, twisting until they were holding hands, returning his squeeze.

He closed his eyes briefly, savouring the feel of her hand in his. He had no idea what was happening to him and as much as it terrified him, it also made him happier than he'd ever been.

Chapter 28

Megan moaned loudly before Dean took possession of her mouth. His fingers were imbedded in her mass of mahogany hair as he moved above her, inside her. They had been like this from the moment the door to her apartment had closed, each no longer able to go on without touching the other.

They had tripped and stumbled down the hall while trying to remove every offending piece of clothing and fell together in a tangled mass of limbs onto the bed before joining in one motion, Megan's hips rising to meet him.

Now they were on the cusp of climax, racing headfirst towards the stars and Megan shivered and tightened before coming completely undone, her entire body shuddering, Dean not far behind her.

As they lay together in the aftermath of their lovemaking, their mingled scents floating around them, Dean thought about the case, about Megan and the future—if there was one—and of Tony and Emma. He tried to remember them as the happy people they'd been and not the bloody corpses he'd last seen.

Megan moved her head so she could look up at him. "Is everything all right?" she asked.

Dean stared down into her green eyes, worry for him reflected in their deep depths. "Of course. Why wouldn't it be?"

She reached up and touched his head. "Because you're thinking way too much. What's going on in there?"

Dean caught her hand and brought it to his lips. "I'm sorry I'm not good at this—relationships. My last one was over two years ago and I wouldn't call that a relationship."

Megan frowned. "What would you call it?"

He shrugged. "Occasional sex."

She flinched. Dean replayed his last words and silently cursed how blunt they'd come out.

"What do you call this?" Megan demanded. "Wait…no. I don't want to know."

She began to sit up, but he grabbed hold of her, rolling over to pin her body between his much larger one and the mattress. He stroked her soft satin hair gently, the scent of vanilla wafting up to tickle his nostrils. His heart turned over. He knew that if he didn't lay everything on the line he was going to lose the best thing that ever happened to him.

"Something special, Megan. Something special. I don't know how else to describe it. I'm not all that great with feelings and acknowledging them. In the army it was considered a weakness. Something we should never show, and I live by that rule even to this day."

He looked away for a second, trying to collect himself before turning back to her. She was listening intently to his words. Her breathing was slow and even. In the dark, her eyes appeared almost black. She didn't push him, and he was thankful for that.

Her hardened nipples poked him with every breath, arousing him even now. He ignored his growing dick, determined to tell Megan his sordid tale. He needed her to understand he wasn't a man of pretty words and why he was that way.

"I was a boy, barely shaving, coming from an academic background. I saw the worst a human being could inflict on another but the worst was watching my friend die. His name was Tony, a shining star. We were together from the start.

"On one of our overseas missions we were captured. A small team of five, including one woman, Emma. The girl Tony was going to marry." Tears filled his eyes and he recalled what they had done to Emma, in full view of their prisoners, things that he couldn't even speak of, certainly not to Megan. It was bad enough he had nightmares. He couldn't give them to her.

"They hurt her." A tear escaped his thinly veiled control and rolled down his cheek.

"They tortured her. Even in the most crowded room I can still hear her screams."

Megan wiped away his tear with her thumb before taking the drop into her mouth. He could see his pain reflected in her eyes. Her heart was aching for him.

"You killed them."

Not a question, and certainly not a judgement. He was thankful. He hated the anti-war activists. Dean had spent his early twenties protecting the country so they had the freedom to protest. Did they think the men and women who signed up wanted war? No. But it was a necessary evil. Just as killing the insurgents had been. There was no bargaining with them, no reasoning. Only death.

He nodded. They'd done more than kill them. "We slaughtered them. Every last one of the sons-of-bitches. But not before they killed Emma, and Tony decided to die right along with her. He loved her and he had to watch her die. I still remember the look of torment on his face. He was completely devastated. I vowed then I'd never be in his position. Never feel."

She swallowed hard and blinked up at him. He was sure she was holding back her own tears. Were they because he'd told her he never wanted to feel—love?

"I'm sorry. I know they're just words and pitiful ones at that. I can't imagine what it must've been like for you. How terrifying. How painful. I'm amazed you got out of there in one piece." She stroked his face gently. "But then you've always been the strong one. The hero."

Dean shook his head. "I'm no hero."

"You're mine. I wish I could be yours," she whispered, but he still heard her, and kissed her lips softly. "It's okay if you're no good at this relationship thing. Clearly, I'm not good at it either. Although my past isn't as tragic, I'm scared too. Of loving. Of needing. We'll muddle through it together. If you agree?"

Dean answered her with a kiss, a long, deep kiss filled with promise and the things he could never say out loud.

He tightened his arm around Megan's form, her naked body pressed against his. He liked knowing he'd possessed that body, had tasted all it had to offer. She meant more to him than anyone or anything had before. He felt a moment of crippling fear before pushing it aside. What was done was done. There was no going back, not that he wanted to. A life without Megan in it wasn't worth living. She was his, now and forever.

He'd never told anyone, not even any of his colleagues or the LAC appointed psychologist, about his time overseas. Yet, it seemed right to tell Megan. He'd wanted her to understand him and why he may not always be the man she deserved.

***

Megan loved the feel of him. All hard muscles. He was utterly breathtaking. Her mouth practically watered at the thought of him. She was insatiable when it came to him. She traced the tattoo of the Australian Defence Force emblem on his chest with her fingertips, feeling his strength.

She'd noticed another tattoo, a sharp looking thorn circling his upper arm, right above the names Tony and Emma in a beautiful italic font. It made sense to her now, knowing the story behind the words. She hurt for him, wishing she could do more to soothe and comfort him as he'd done for her, but she knew nothing of his world—couldn't even begin to understand it—so anything she might say would be hollow.

She'd thought she was the only one who feared falling in love. Not because of commitment. She had no trouble with that. It was the giving your heart to another person part that made her panic. The thought of loving someone so much that you'd die beside them, preferring death to living without them, terrified her. What if she loved like that and lost him? She would be completely shattered.

It was ironic. She wrote romance novels for a living. She always sought the happy ending, but in a novel, love was safe. It wasn't real. No one could be hurt or lost.

She remembered her mother and how she'd been after her father died. A shell of her former self. She simply hadn't wanted to go on living, so she'd stopped. She'd left Megan alone to follow her husband into the great unknown. Megan hoped they were together again. It made the abandonment hurt less.

"I honestly don't know what this is. Or even if it can become more. I just know I need it…that I need you, Megan."

Her heart sped up. His words were the most romantic ones she'd ever heard or written while at the same time not intending to be.

"I feel the same way."

"So we're in agreement. We see where this leads. But no promises."

"Agreed."

She wasn't going to tell him or even admit it to

herself that it might already be too late. She could only hope he changed his mind before her heart was irrevocably broken.

Already she was spiralling headfirst towards a sea of emotion she'd not felt before and part of her was fighting it. She liked Dean. Enjoyed his company and certainly his sexual prowess, but she didn't want to love him even though she was sure she was well past that stage. Her stomach flipped when she saw him, her heart beating a bit faster as he came towards her. If she allowed him into her heart—her soul—would she be able to keep on going if something happened to him?

She forced her mind away from those thoughts. Now was not the time to worry over them. She had Dean in her bed and she was sure she could find plenty of pleasurable things to do.

She ran her hand over his impressive pecs and abs. They made her feel inadequate. A man like that could get any number of gorgeous women, so why would he want her?

She'd never been insecure about her body until she saw the magnificent condition he kept his in. She was no slouch. She hated gyms and any form of exercise. But she practiced Yoga almost daily when she wasn't preoccupied with writing. That and sometimes she skipped meals when she was too absorbed in her work.

Unable to stop herself, she leaned over him and licked his chest. She swirled her tongue over his muscles, delighting in the texture and taste. She slid down his body, kissing him as she went. He shifted beneath her exploration and let out an unsteady breath. She liked having power over him—at least in the bedroom. It gave her a rush that she could pleasure a man like Dean Matthews.

She reached his groin and pressed a kiss to the head. His chocolate eyes glittered in the dark, the moonlight peeking through the open venetian blinds, catching the irises. His hips arched as she took him into her mouth, her tongue grazing over the sensitive underside. She grasped the base with her fist and exerted pressure as she worked him, relaxing her throat to take him deeper. He groaned harshly as she let go of him to cup his sac. He was close. Just a little more…

He halted her, slipping from her mouth. She made a sound of protest.

"I want you to come with me," he told her raggedly.

She smiled seductively and licked her lips slowly as she stared into his eyes. Holding him captive, she straddled him and scooped up the foil packet from the bed side table and rolled it over his length, teasing him with her fingertips as she did so. When he was sheathed she raised herself and settled over him.

A moment later he was inside her, filling her. She gasped at the sensation of him expanding inside her. She moved her hips and he let out a groan.

His smoky chocolate gaze devoured her as she rode him and left her breathless. Her breasts bounced as he thrust into her and she let out a small scream. She wasn't going to last much longer. She was already on the cusp of an orgasm.

She panted, wanting to make it last.

"Are you close?" he asked between clenched teeth.

She nodded and was sure she'd made some sound of agreement.

"Come with me, Meg."

He'd barely touched her clit before she was climaxing. Her world darkened and spun on its axis and she screamed his name as her body shook and shuddered. She became boneless and collapsed over his broad chest. His strong arms wrapped around her and held tight. Dean pressed a kiss to her head and her heart clenched. She was quickly falling for him. There wasn't a part of him she didn't like. Yes, she was totally falling in love with the man, *dammit*.

She kissed his chest again, feeling his strong heartbeat beneath her fingertips. If there was ever a man to lose herself to, it would be Dean Matthews. She only hoped she didn't live to regret it. Finally accepting her fate, she closed her eyes and fell into an easy sleep.

Chapter 29

He watched the woman—more a girl than woman—stagger towards her beat-up 1990 Toyota Corolla. Her high heels added four inches to her height. How did she walk in them? Not that it mattered to him; he was just curious. He waited in his pickup as she tripped against the car.

His gaze searched the area, carefully cataloguing his surroundings, the late night shoppers stopping in at the local convenience store for the next day's bread and milk, the two giggling teenage girls crossing the road, the time of night telling him they'd snuck out. His fingers itched to give them a lesson in obeying their parents, that the dark night was no time to be out alone, but he couldn't. They would be missed by morning and he knew they'd be no fun, absolutely no fun at all.

He turned his attention from the silly girls begging for trouble and back at his mark who was currently fighting with her door, trying to get it open. The door was stuck and after another minute she gave up, stalking over to the passenger side and jerking it open. After hiking up her already short skirt, she climbed over the centre console, then turned the key in the ignition and he could smell the petrol burning, dark smoke exited the muffler as she revved the overused engine, which protested loudly at being woken up from a well-deserved break. She flicked on her lights, the left rear break light busted, leaving only the red glare from the right.

She backed out of her parking spot, sending him awash with a dull white light. He reached over and started his own engine, following her out of the lot and into traffic where he kept two car lengths behind her the entire way until she stopped outside a large apartment building that seemed like home to this woman.

Pulling up at the kerb across from where she'd parked, he waited for her to exit the car, practically falling out of the vehicle. Yes. She was ripe for the picking. Almost as if she wanted him to take her away from her pitiful life in which she sold her lovely but useless body every night. He'd seen her take several men into the alley beside the store.

He was getting antsy. He'd gotten rid of the last one days ago. She'd disappointed him. He found he was tiring of them quickly, none of them living up to his expectations and now he wanted—needed—another. He swiped his sweaty hands against his slacks and calmed his racing heart.

He smiled grimly into the dark enclosure of his vehicle. The air outside was warm, slowly seeping through the rust cracks of the panelling. There was no moon tonight, no light except for the bare bulb of the occasional streetlight that wasn't blown. The light not enough to make out more than a few feet in front of his face. The apartment building was dark, probably used as a squatter location rather than a renters' market. He opened the door to his car and was assaulted by the horrid, rank scent of rodents.

He stood on the rough potholed asphalt that was years too late for a revamp, the council having forgotten this part of town. Hell, even when Coleani had ruled, the neighbourhood hadn't been in this bad of disarray. He thought briefly of the crime boss who'd owned half the city before the police had shot him and destroyed his empire.

He moved slowly, not just because of his limp—the result of a beating gone bad in his youth—but because he didn't want to make any noise, alerting her to his presence. He wanted to take her by surprise. He hated it when they struggled. The last one almost knocked him off his feet. His boots made almost no sound as he approached her. Within a minute, he'd caught up to her. She had ditched the heels, carrying them in her hands by the straps and for that he was thankful, because there was nothing more painful than a heel in his instep. He grabbed her from behind, his arms immediately cutting off her air supply as he jerked her against him.

Her fingernails dug into his skin leaving half-moon shapes as crimson swelled around the marks and he drew in a sharp breath, his other hand moving from her stomach to her wrist. He applied pressure, almost enough to break it but only bruising the delicate bones. She gasped and swallowed hard and he guessed right about now she was seeing the sweet stars that came before the darkness, of the blessed unconsciousness that often swirled around the edges of his mind. He envied her just a bit as he sent her there, her limbs going slack against him, her skin turning a slight shade of blue. He reached down, hooking his arm beneath her legs and lifted her into his arms. Looking about the area, he walked back to his car, ever vigilant, the extra weight slowing him down. He stuffed her into the boot of his car before slamming it shut and climbed back behind the wheel. He took his time, not wanting to draw any attention to himself.

He wasn't worried about someone finding her car. Even if they did, he doubted the car was registered and if it was, the likelihood it was in her name was slim. Besides what could they do with a name? Hadn't experience told him the police were useless? He had been doing this for some time. Carolyn Harper had not been his first. Unfortunately, the animals hadn't picked her clean, but ten months later they were still no closer to finding him. Nevertheless, he had to be cautious. He couldn't afford to make mistakes.

He turned a corner carefully. Within a half hour, he was pulling up outside his home, just twenty kilometres outside of the city's bounds, off the King George Highway. He knew it wasn't smart to dump his victims so close to home, but he liked knowing they were nearby.

A groan emanating from the boot told him his victim was slowly regaining consciousness. He had to move fast. He didn't want a fight on his hands. He preferred to be passive, to watch the women fight to get out, tearing their skin until it was hanging off the bone, their fingernails torn and bloody. The very thought gave him the sensation of pleasure, so intense it felt like a sucker punch to the stomach.

He opened the trunk, his feet braced apart, in preparation for a struggle but none was forthcoming. He lifted her and carried her into the house where she would wake up to a nightmare.

Chapter 30

The door closed behind Dean and the silence was its own form of torture. When Dean was around, Megan's whole world seemed to narrow until there were only the two of them and the horrors of her life melted away. Now, he was gone, and Megan found herself at the doorway to Stacey's room staring at the reminders of her cousin. The things Stacey cared about. Though the past few days had been some of her best, guilt had been a blossoming pit inside her, condemning her for being happy when her cousin was still lost. What type of person was she that she cared more for her own happiness than her cousin's safety?

Feeling unsettled, she refused to allay her concerns to Dean, knowing he was doing all he could. She would not add to his burden.

She could see the stress of the case in the lines on his face and in his eyes. Megan owed him for being her rock, his strength making her strong when she would've been weak. Without him, Megan knew she'd have been a crumbling mess.

Closing her eyes, she breathed in deeply, searching for calm while her scattered emotions caused chaos in her mind and body. For a second, Megan caught Stacey's lingering scent and her stomach lurched.

"I miss you, Stacey. Please come home safe."

When the phone rang, she raced for it, hope overriding her better senses as she wished it were Stacey. Her socks slid along the hardwood floors before she came to a stop beside the kitchen counter. Her heart sank and her mood slipped deeper into darkness when she heard her aunt's voice on the other end.

"Why hasn't Stacey been found?" she barked. "Why aren't you helping? Don't you want her to come home?" The barrage of questions were like a knife in her heart, each slice accurate with its ability to cause pain.

Sinking to the floor, her knees buckling under strain, Megan hugged one arm around her raised knees. Her aunt's voice, filled with worry, chipped at her already delicate state. When she tried to explain, Cathy hung up and Megan heard the deafening silence.

She should be doing more. But how? Dean and the LAC were doing all they could. She wasn't the character in her book who took charge and solved cases. Surely they had all the angles covered. Her problem was she didn't know nearly enough about the case or the killer. She couldn't ask Dean and she refused to go to Amelia. It wouldn't be fair on either of them.

Who else could she turn to for help?

Forty minutes later, she was standing in the foyer of the local news station.

***

When he heard her name on the television in the Command Centre, Dean frowned and listened closely. The news anchor spoke, introducing the cousin of the missing teen. A moment later, Megan appeared and looking directly into the camera, pleaded for Stacey's safe return.

His team members were also riveted to the screen and seemed to be gauging his response. A sharp pain stabbed at his heart as Megan spoke about the case, mentioning details they'd wanted to keep quiet. He'd only told her those things because he trusted her. As his stomach roiled and he felt his face flush, he began to think trusting her had been a grave mistake.

Amelia came to stand beside him. "I take it you didn't know about this?"

"No." His jaw clenched. "Since you're here asking me, I'm guessing she didn't run this past you either?"

"I'd have told her not to bother if she had. The Highway Dumper hasn't shown any interest in returning or even ransoming his victims. I don't believe money interests him."

"All she's doing is making our life harder by having every crackpot in the city calling up in hopes of getting that reward money she's offering."

His eye twitched. Why the hell hadn't she told him her plans? She clearly didn't have much faith in his abilities or in him. After last night, he'd been sure they'd made progress in their relationship. This incident told him it hadn't meant as much to Megan as it did him.

Betrayal, thick and heavy, seemed to suffocate him. His throat tightened, and he felt his vision narrow as adrenaline jumpstarted his pulse, making it beat frantically. Had Megan used him to gather information? Yesterday, he'd not have thought it possible. Today, with the evidence before him, he couldn't see another answer. An emotion he couldn't name made his heart ache. His face burning, Dean couldn't stand still. His body was primed for a fight and he knew just where he wanted to let it loose. God help Megan Bailey, because he longer cared what she thought or how she felt. *Not giving a shit is my only option.* Did he truly not care, or was he just veiling his feelings with fury?

"Dean, wait." When he didn't stop or slow down, Nick chased after him, but nothing his partner said or did would stop him from confronting her.

Chapter 31

"Dean, what are you doing here?" Megan glanced uneasily at the man she thought she knew, who was now glowering at her in a way she'd never expected. She stopped in the corridor of the news station just a few feet from him. He looked seriously pissed. Reservations filled her and had her questioning her actions, but it was too late.

"The more important question is, what the fuck are you doing here? You just jeopardised the entire fucking case."

The harshness of his tone sliced across her heart and she stepped back, trying to ignore the pain. She glanced at Nick, who stood behind him, and when he appeared to ignore her, she focused on Dean again.

She ran her palm nervously over the denim of her jeans.

"I thought I could help. I never intended to do harm. Aunt Cathy said I wasn't doing enough. She was right. How I can I sit at home and live my life when Stacey is out there?"

His voice was little more than a growl. "Yeah, well, you probably just killed her."

Megan reeled, black dots appearing in her vision. Light-headed, she swayed until she heard Nick telling her to breathe. She gulped in a lungful of air. How could he say those things?

She heard Nick reprimand his partner, but the man's demeanour didn't change. Megan pressed her hand against her chest and breathed deep, stabilising herself. Glancing up, she found him staring at her as if they'd never been lovers—as if she didn't matter.

"You bastard." She forced the words out of her mouth, her knees weak. She wasn't sure she'd be able to remain standing, but somehow she did. Maybe she was stronger than she felt.

How could he say that to her? Why would he do this?

"How long have you been planning this?"

She frowned, unsure what he meant. The question wasn't as simple as it sounded.

"Just…since this morning. I had to do something, Dean."

She implored him to understand, to be the man she needed right now when she felt so lost. She needed her lover, not the cop who stood before her, but she feared she'd lost him because of her rash actions. But how could a plea for help do more damage than good?

"You didn't tell me because you knew what you were doing was wrong."

She wasn't sure, but she began to think they were having two separate conversations.

She shifted on her feet and straightened, taking a

deep breath. "I didn't tell you because I didn't want you to talk me out of it. If there's even the slightest hope that it might help, I had to do it."

His eyes burned in fury. "You don't trust me, is that it?"

Nick stood close to them both, silent. A woman in a business suit came through the front door of the station and bypassed them hurriedly, as if sensing the tension.

Desperation had her insides twisting in panic. "That's not what this is about. You of all people should understand how helpless I feel."

His nostrils flared and his lips compressed into a tight line. "You're going to throw that back at me?" She had the feeling she'd said the wrong thing, while only trying to have him understand her reasoning. Stepping forward, she reached for him. Dean caught her wrists. "If you need something to do, write another damn book."

He pushed her back lightly and released her hands, his gentle actions at war with his words and manner.

Megan's own temper flared as her back straightened.

"What would you have me do, Dean? What would you have done in my position?" Crushing disappointment had her shoulders sagging. "It's fine for you. You're out there doing stuff. I can't sit idly by."

"I wouldn't use someone to get what I want."

Her head jerked back. "What the hell are you talking about?"

"You're giving away things I told you in

confidence."

"You never told me that. I thought you were sharing common knowledge. How was I supposed to know it wasn't to be shared?" A hysterical laugh threatened to break free. "Seriously, you thought I'd sleep with you to gather intel so I could do…what, exactly?"

If that's what he believed, what were *his* reasons? Was anything that passed between them real? He hadn't promised her anything, yet she'd allowed her hormones to get the better of her.

"I was always only going to be temporary, wasn't I?"

A part of her died when he said nothing, just stared down at her as though he'd been wronged, not her. That was her answer.

She wasn't sure where to go from there.

"You wanted the truth, Megan. There it is."

A ball of tension tightened inside her. After everything they'd shared, how could he so easily dismiss her? Last night, she'd felt closer to him than she'd ever felt to another human being. Now, his words were cruel, meant to hurt.

She understood pain and holding back. She'd get through this. "I appreciate your honesty, Detective Matthews." With that, she held her head high and walked hurriedly out of the TV station, refusing to break down in front of him.

***

Dean made it to the footpath outside the building, his angry strides eating up twice as much distance before he abruptly turned, searching the parking lot for Megan, determined to find her.

Now, he was angry with himself.

Nick blocked his path. He'd almost forgotten his partner was there.

"What are you doing?" He held his gaze.

"I have to apologise."

"Yeah, but not now. Not while it's so fresh. Give her time to calm down. Give yourself time."

"I was an arsehole."

"Yes. You were. I kept my mouth shut in there, but now that we're alone, I'll say you judged her unfairly."

He'd been quick to condemn her. Why? He was the happiest he'd been when around her.

"I was cruel to her. I don't know why."

Nick studied him. "I think you do know, but you're not ready to hear it."

He chose to ignore Nick's comment, instead desperately glancing over his shoulder, looking for her. She'd already left. Megan was bound to hate him and for good reason. Anger had fuelled his words. Fear that he wasn't what Megan needed or wanted had made him lash out. He was irritated she'd done something without consulting him, making his work that much harder.

Unfair? Yes. Unreasonable? Of course. It didn't change the turbulent emotions swirling dangerously inside him. He only had himself to blame. He'd opened himself up to her and paid the price.

Yeah, that's what pissed him off the most. She hadn't trusted in him enough to tell him her fears and feelings. But then, he'd never been good at sharing emotions.

He realised he wasn't the only one paying the price. He'd crushed her, watched the light extinguish in her eyes when she saw him for the bastard he'd always been.

His heart and brain were in battle. One told him to apologise now and the other said to hold off.

He reluctantly agreed with Nick, and they headed back to the LAC.

Chapter 32

Unable to stomach going home to an empty apartment, Megan drove around aimlessly. In the back of her mind she felt as though she'd betrayed both Dean and Amelia. She couldn't lean on her friend, feeling that would be inappropriate due to Dean being her subordinate and she didn't want to burden Riley. Her next choice would've been Stacey, had she been available. In the end, she couldn't face anyone after what she'd done.

She'd ruined the only relationship she ever cared about in one afternoon. No matter how good her intentions had been, the result was still the same. Her whole body felt numb. She needed to drown her sorrows and forget her troubles, even for a few hours.

Applying the parking brake, she wasn't surprised to find herself outside of Tanner's. Maybe she needed to feel close to Dean, to hold on to that connection.

Ordering her drink from the bar, she slid into the booth she'd sat in with him the last time they were

216

there. So much had changed since then. She was in love with a man who hated her. Sipping her drink, she avoided making eye contact and hid in the corner, replaying the last few hours.

He hadn't called her. She supposed that deep down she'd known he wouldn't. In his mind, she was only the family member of a victim. Would he be the one to tell her when they found Stacey, or would he send Nick instead? Biting her lip, Megan tried to ignore the pain consuming all the happiness she'd felt, replacing it with despair.

Should she track him down and apologise?

Something told her he wouldn't appreciate seeing her now. Though she believed his actions were unreasonable, Megan would do anything to remove the distance growing between them and obtain his forgiveness.

One rash action had the ability to ruin everything.

Could she be more pitiful?

Burying her head in her arms, she breathed in the strong scents of aged beer that permeated the wooden table top. Her stomach rolled for another reason.

A waitress stopped by and collected her empty glass. "Can I get you another?"

"Thanks. That'll be good."

The young woman was back in a couple minutes with another drink. "Hey, don't I know you? You were here with a couple of the guys from the LAC, right?"

Megan read the woman's name tag. **'Glory'**. She remembered her and tried to drum up some enthusiasm, but her delivery fell flat.

"I've never seen anyone look so bleak," Glory said. "And I hang out with world weary cops all the time. Man troubles?"

Tears welled in her eyes. She blinked them back furiously.

The woman surprised her by sitting down and placing her hand over Megan's, gently squeezing her fingers. "It can't be all that bad, can it?"

To her embarrassment, a tear rolled down her cheek. She swiped it away, ducking her head. She hated crying in public. In hindsight, coming to a bar probably wasn't the brightest idea. Yet another bad decision.

Misery overrode all her other emotions, and a heavy feeling sank in the pit of her stomach, refusing to budge. This morning had started off so optimistically. She'd woken up in Dean's arms, and now all of that was shattered.

Why'd I let Aunt Cathy get to me? If anything happened to her cousin, she would never forgive herself. Nor would she forget how she'd been the one to destroy her connection with Dean.

"I think I just ruined my only chance at happiness."

"You're going to need another drink," Glory said.

Megan didn't argue. A couple of drinks later, her head felt fuzzy.

The waitress tried her best to lift her spirits, and they shared a few laughs, but her troubles were always in the back of mind, ready to spring when the laughter died down. She yawned, her eyelids

218

heavy, and with great difficulty she reopened them to focus on the sauce bottle in the centre of the table.

"You're officially cut off," Glory said.

Megan shrugged. "I'm a cheap drunk. I suppose I should be getting home."

But to what? The isolation depressed her. Maybe she would harass Riley and camp out on her couch.

"I'm not letting you drive out of here in this condition."

"I'll call a cab." She dug through her purse only to come up empty. "I must've left my phone in the car."

"I'll call you a cab from the bar phone."

"Thanks. I'll go wait by my car."

She swayed on her feet as she said goodbye to the waitress. Only stumbling once, she made it to her car and pressed the unlock button on her key fob. Grasping her phone, she heard someone approach.

"Found it," she said to Glory, triumphant.

When the waitress didn't response, the hairs on the back of her neck rose and a ripple of unease rolled over her. She moved back, but it was already too late. The presence boxed her in and someone grabbed her from behind, lifting her off the ground. Her legs flailed about, her feet striking out at anything it touched, denting the side panel of her car. Her scream was cut off by a large hand over her mouth, overwhelming her, and nothing she did had any effect against the hard body holding her so tightly.

A hard object rammed into her body and a

painful jolt soared through her bloodstream. The world went black around her, her body seizing with each electric jab.

This is the man who took Stacey.

She sobbed, fear overriding her senses as she slipped into unconsciousness.

Chapter 33

The next day, Dean stood inside the Harbour Bay Medical Centre as he waited for his escort, a young Pakistani doctor dressed in his impeccably white coat. The doctor approached warily, noting the badge and holster clipped to his belt.

Dean held out his hand and the doctor shook it. "Thank you for seeing me. I understand this is somewhat of an unusual time of day for an interview, but believe me, time is of the essence."

"Of course, however I can help," the doctor replied in perfect English.

Dean nodded. The medical centre was a hub of activity, even in the early hours of the morning. A woman dressed in a navy blue apron walked past pushing a mop and bucket, her dark hair pulled into a bun at the base of her neck.

He'd been unable to sleep. He couldn't stop thinking about the fight at the TV station, and he felt a tightness around his heart. Something else nagged at him incessantly. Without Megan clouding his mind, he'd be able to focus on finding that last missing piece of the puzzle. He was so close, but something eluded him.

He'd stared at the map of the city in the Command Centre until he was sure his eyes had crossed. The map resembled a pin cushion, each pin marking the site where each of the victims had last been seen and where the bodies had been recovered. He'd reviewed the radius around the dots, the hunting ground where the Highway Dumper felt comfortable. The neighbourhood was still referred to as Coleani's, a part of town that birthed crime, drugs, and prostitution along with every other illegal activity. For years it had been a cesspool but was slowly returning to its former glory.

He'd stared so hard at the map that he'd almost missed it. The small symbol in the middle of the Highway Dumper's comfort zone, a place where the victims would go for medical treatment, drugs, and contraception. They wouldn't be able to shell out the big bucks for a doctor's visit but the centre was bulk billed—one of the few places that still did it in the city.

A place that was sure to stock SNP.

Which is how he'd ended up at the medical centre at barely seven in the morning. "Do you usually run the night shift?" His body pulsed as he recognised the signs of excitement at knowing he was on the right track. *Finally.*

"It varies. Sometimes I do the days or evenings. We all take turns."

"But you know the people that worked those shifts correct?"

"Of course. We are a small medical centre. It

requires a lot of teamwork to keep functional."

"I'm looking for a man. Someone who doesn't have a lot of responsibility. Someone who isn't around much but has access to your drug cabinets. Do you by chance have any Sodium Nitroprusside in your supply?"

The doctor frowned. "Yes. We have some for emergency heart cases, to treat hypertension."

"Can I please see your supply?"

If the doctor thought it an unusual request, he didn't say anything. Dean assumed he must see a lot of things that weren't of the norm. Running a medical centre, he supposed, meant you'd see your fair share of whack jobs.

Dean followed the doctor down one hall and into another, coming to a stop at a door. The doctor reached into his pocket and withdrew his keys, finding the right one and put it into the lock. With one twist, the door was open and Dean was standing in a small office, bare except for one desk, chair, and an out of date computer.

"This room is used to control the drugs entering and exiting the centre. When they come in, when they go out, how much and by who."

"And you've had none of your drugs missing?"

The doctor shook his head as he opened the only other object in the room—a door. "No, not to my knowledge, and as you can see we run a very tight ship. If memory serves, one of my colleagues had a call from a detective asking about missing drugs. The answer was the same."

"Yes. That would've been my partner, but now we have new information to go on and unfortunately, your clinic is in the middle of it."

Dean stepped inside the supply room. It was a closet more than a room, with stainless steel shelves stocked to the point of overfilling. It was a druggie's wet dream. He glanced at some of the names printed on the bottles and didn't recognise most of them, but the ones he saw could be dangerous in the wrong hands. He found the Sodium Nitroprusside and glanced at the small glass bottle. It looked as innocuous as one might expect, but Dean was sure he was on the right track.

"Find what you're looking for?"

"Not yet." He studied the bottle. It hadn't been opened and none appeared to be missing, but he was absolutely certain this was the batch that helped kill six women.

"May I see it?" the doctor asked, and Dean handed the bottle to him. He studied the glass container just as he had, frowning.

"What is it?"

"I'm not sure, but it's strange." The doctor stepped up to the shelves and searched for something. He pulled out another glass bottle the same size and studied the level of liquid in each. "Oh my goodness."

Dean moved closer, trying to see what the doctor saw. He reached into the box of Sodium Nitroprusside and brought out another glass container and then another. Dean had finally found what he was looking for, and the result was not good. If only they'd had known about the chemical compound earlier. Maybe they'd have been able to prevent the deaths.

"How much would you say is missing?"

"Hardly any. A few millimetres."

Dean counted the glass bottles. There were ten altogether. "So we're looking at what…twenty millimetres of the drug gone?"

The doctor paled and nodded at the same time.

"Okay…who has access?"

***

Dean was back in his car before the call had gone through. Nick answered before the third ring. Dean didn't bother wasting time.

"His name is Clayton Brady and he lives on Hudson."

"Who? The Highway Dumper?" Nick asked, his tone incredulous.

"Yeah."

"Holy shit, Dean. How'd you find that out?"

"Unimportant. Just meet me there. I'm already on my way." He pulled out into the traffic that had begun to pick up. He'd spent over an hour in the medical centre but he'd hit pay dirt.

"Hudson's just over the highway, isn't it? Farm land?"

"Yeah. King George Highway."

Twenty minutes later, he was slowing his car to a stop and was out of his seat, his Ray-Ban sunglasses perched on his nose, blocking out the harsh UV rays that promised the day would be a scorcher. He sat down on the hood as Nick along with the rest of their team pulled up.

"I've got a couple of uniforms setting up a

225

barricade. I counted at least four different ways off this road," Nick told him as he walked towards him, already wearing his bullet-proof vest. He stared down the narrow one-car road with contempt. "Clayton Brady owns number 604. He inherited it after his mother died."

Darryl, James, and Matt were all dressed in the same navy blue vest with **'POLICE'** stamped in white on the back. Dean moved to the boot of his car removing his own and shrugged into it as Nick detailed the plan of attack.

"604 is located on the left. There are two farmhouses located nearby. One just across the road and the other to the right of his property. We'll split up, each taking an entrance."

They didn't bother to warn each other about a potential hostage. They all knew the stakes were high. It wasn't their first ambush. They knew what needed to be done and how to avoid problems if they could. There was a small chance Stacey Bailey was somewhere in the house, and it made the situation tense.

"Okay, let's do this. Approach on foot. I don't want to warn this fuck. Hopefully, we'll catch him snoring." Matt withdrew his weapon.

Darryl spoke into his radio, informing dispatch and the uniforms on the boundaries what was about to happen, in hopes of limiting the surprised or itchy trigger fingers.

Dean moved out, jogging along the dirt road before stepping into the nearby tree line, disappearing completely from view. Nick followed suit, signalling to James.

They each spread out, taking their time to surround the decaying farmhouse. Dean took position, crawling towards the house, staying beneath the view line and placing his back to the house, beneath a window. He turned his head, looking through the dirty window at the near deserted house. He couldn't see anyone, but his training was telling him it wasn't deserted. A moment later it was confirmed when he heard a floorboard creak.

Dean listened to his team as they spoke into his earpiece. One by one they took their positions at the entrances and exits of the house.

A glass broke inside the house and a woman screamed. Dean heard Matt's command "Go!" and bolted into action. A moment later the window was broken and he was inside, easily manoeuvring thorough the unusual surroundings. His gun was out in front of him, his finger resting on the trigger guard. Sounds of wood splintering and glass breaking came from every direction as his team joined him.

Dean scanned the room, looking for signs of life and movement. He crossed the room, clearing it, and came to the doorway and quickly stuck his head into the line of fire before retreating, his brain registering the layout, informing him there was no immediate danger.

He moved into the kitchen, noting the broken glass on the floor along with what appeared to be juice. He scanned the area, looking for the person who'd been in the room just seconds ago. He stepped forward, his body calm. It was his job to function in highly stressful scenarios in which lives were held in the balance.

Dean couldn't hear his team move around and that was the way it should be. No man worth his salt would ever allow himself to be heard, even by his allies. Like a magician, he never gave up his secrets not even to another magician.

He took another step, then another before he heard the faint rustling nearby. He moved towards it, keeping his senses open in case it was a trap, leading him away from his real prize. He navigated around the window, not allowing a shadow to be cast as he moved and reached out for the doorknob twisting it quickly as he pushed it away from him.

The room before him was dark, the curtain closed, but that wasn't Dean's main problem. His problem was from the growl he heard emanate from the room. His finger immediately moved to the trigger as a large Doberman, teeth bared, skin pulled back, emerged from the darkness. He leaned on his front legs in a gesture Dean knew all too well. *Mother fucker*, he thought as the dog launched itself into the air. He squeezed the trigger and the animal fell to floor with a loud thud. He heard footsteps and turned his weapon to the newest threat, remaining weary when an old woman appeared, still dressed in a long nightgown. She caught sight of her dog and screamed.

"What have you done?" she sobbed.

Dean lowered his weapon to the floor. He could see Darryl and James coming up behind the woman, their weapons ready to take action should the woman prove to be hostile.

"Ma'am, is this your house?"

"Of course this is my house. You shot my dog!"

He felt bad about that, but if it came down to a dog or a human, he always knew who would come out on top. "Are you alone? Ma'am, are you alone?" he repeated, the woman's face locked onto her dog.

"Yes, goddamn it, yes."

"What is the number of this house?" He sensed movement near him and his gun was once more ready.

"No, don't hurt him," the woman yelled as her dog tried to move, whimpering in pain. He ignored the guilt at shooting an animal. He'd make it right later.

"The house number, what is it?" he demanded.

"614."

"Fuck," Dean said, jerking his head to the side, telling Darryl and James to move out. He followed them.

Chapter 34

Clayton Brady watched the screen before him. These were his favourite times, when the girl tried to claw her way out. His body tightened with anticipation, knowing that her life could end at any time. All he had to do was pour his lethal mixture onto the dry ice in the air filter and wait until the caustic vapour reached her. He smiled. He couldn't wait for that part. Maybe he could just do it now? Oh, what fun it would be. More fun than watching the woman try to get out. She was useless, after all. Expendable.

As he moved his hand towards his glass of water, the unmistakable sound of the safety being removed from a gun filled his ears.

"Move an inch and your brains will be all over this room."

No, this wasn't right. Surely, he must be dreaming. There was no way the cops could have found him. There was no leads. No evidence. What was happening? The detective reached down and jerked him to his feet, slamming him up against the wall.

"Where is she?"

He laughed. He would never give up his hiding place. Not even if they broke every bone in his body. He could withstand pain. Mother had taught him well.

Brown eyes filled with contempt glared at him before pushing him away. "Get this sad fuck out of my face!"

He struggled, wanting to watch the bitch just a little while longer. She was close to panicking now and that was always fun to witness but suddenly he was out of his house, into the yard he had played in as a child before his mother had taken everything he loved away from him.

He was stuffed into the backseat of a car—not just any car. A police car. All around, people milled about, snapping photos and putting up crime tape. No, this was his house. All his. He was the one to endure all the pain and suffering at the hands of mother, no one else. No one was entitled to that house.

He started to scream at them to get off his property, to leave him alone, but no one paid any attention to him. This was not right. He had spent his entire youth praying to God that just once, his mother would forget about him, would not see him, but it never happened. Wherever he was, whatever he was doing, she'd always find him and that was when the pain began.

Now he couldn't get one person to look at him. Had his prayers finally been answered? Was he finally invisible? He raged at the men and women on his lawn but not one looked his way. He glared at them all. *They'll see*. He'd find a way to come back and make each of them pay.

He heard the crackle of a radio and turned around. A young police officer with ginger hair was driving the car, taking him away from his home, taking him to where the bad men would try to hurt him. But they'd see. No one could hurt him. He was immune.

***

Dean stared at the small monitor on the table as the woman moved about the room, clawing at the walls and he swallowed back the nausea. The bastard had watched his victims die, had watched them try to escape knowing full well that in the end, he was the one who made that decision.

"Find where the feed is," he demanded.

A young tech immediately connected his Netbook with the farmhouse's wireless feed. "She'll have to be close."

He nodded before stalking out of the room and locating Nick who was directing the uniforms in a grid by grid search. A shout from the other side of the house had him running towards the sound and Dean saw the small blacked out window almost hidden underneath overgrown weeds. Within seconds a path was cleared and he stood staring at a wood door bolted shut. Soon they had the bolt on the ground, broken in two pieces, and a wall of bricks stood between him and possibly Stacey.

"The fucker sealed the room."

Matt, James, and Darryl joined him, each brandishing a crow bar. He stepped back. "By all means."

Together the three men broke through the wall.

He climbed through the broken bricks, looking around at the small claustrophobic room. There was mould in the air and he coughed as it settled in his lungs. A young girl huddled in the corner, her hands held protectively over her face. He moved towards her and he could see the skin of her fingers almost hanging from the bones having been shredded against the rough brick walls. She shied away from him and his heart sank.

He knelt down in front of her, his voice soothing when he spoke. "It's okay, you're all right. He's gone. He can't hurt you anymore."

A sob exited a pouty mouth and tears left a wet track through the dirt on her face, her hand shaking as she brought it her forehead.

"I've been so scared," her gravelly voice whispered.

"I know, but it's okay. There's an ambulance outside ready to take you to the hospital."

"He took me, locked me away. He didn't even talk me no matter how much I begged."

He reached out gently, bringing the girl into his arms. A girl who wasn't Stacey but needed his help just as much if not more. It was clear her mind wasn't strong, the traumatic event close to breaking her. Would she recover or was this the beginning of a downward spiral? The girl came willingly, most likely seeking out something tangible that would tell her it wasn't a dream, that she was safe. He breathed through his mouth as he stroked the matted hair.

Behind him, he could hear his team continuing to remove bricks, making the hole wider, not just for him but for the forensic team that would be required to collect evidence and take photos.

The girl's petite body shook. Her bones almost protruded from her skin and he knew she hadn't been in the best shape prior to her abduction, another lost soul the Highway Dumper—Clayton Brady—had preyed upon.

"What's your name?"

She swallowed hard. "L-Lucy W-Webber."

"Nice to meet you, Lucy Webber. Do you have any family I can call? Have them meet you at the hospital?"

She shook her head. "No. All alone." She started crying again, her sobs causing her whole body to shake.

"Shhh, rest."

He stood, slipped an arm beneath her legs and carried her towards the sun. She soon wouldn't be alone. She was the Highway Dumper's only surviving victim, and she'd be an overnight sensation. Whether that would help or hinder her was yet to be seen. As he approached the gap in the bricks, Matt reached out to them.

"Go with this detective, Lucy. He'll take good care of you," he said in a low voice, not wanting to scare her as he passed her through the hole and into Matt's open arms. After securing her, Matt turned and headed for the ambulance.

Half an hour later, he leaned against the bonnet

of the car and watched the activity surrounding them. They had saved a life, brought a killer to justice, but he wasn't feeling good about his day. The thought of telling Megan was terrifying. He'd hoped with all his heart that this day would not come. But there was no denying that he'd failed her. The possibility that Stacey was dead was extremely probable.

Nick kicked at a small rock. "I'm sorry, Dean. I know you wanted her to be Stacey. Hell, we all wanted her to be Stacey."

Dean nodded. A heavy feeling settled in his stomach as the ambulance pulled away. "You win some, you lose some. We didn't do too badly. We got one girl. It's only a matter of time before we get the other."

He only wished he felt as optimistic as he sounded.

They were soon joined by Darryl who glared at the swarm of news reporters that had finally showed up. He, like the rest of the team, didn't appreciate being harangued and detested microphones being shoved in his face.

"Those people have no scruples. Bloody vultures, the lot of them. What are you still doing here? I thought you'd want to be the one to interview Brady. After all, you're the one been chasing him this whole time."

"I know he's guilty. What else is there to say?"

"Maybe to learn what he did with Stacey?"

Nick rubbed the back of his neck. "You're assuming she's dead."

Darryl shrugged. "I honestly don't know. But

we're never going to know the answers if the questions are never asked."

Dean let out a deep breath. "I guess I'm scared what those answers will be. Right now I have the luxury of believing she's out there somewhere, alive. But if it does turn out differently, if that bastard touched her—" They all knew where he was going with this.

Darryl stared out into the distance, his gaze unfocused. "If you want, any one of us would be more than happy to take this one."

Dean straightened from the car. "I'm good. I've never backed down from a fight and I'm not going to start now."

Finding Stacey alive would be a fight. A fight to the death.

Chapter 35

Dean glared at Clayton Brady, the Highway Dumper. The man's wrists were handcuffed to the stainless steel table in front of him. He stared at Dean with soulless grey eyes. And that was exactly what he was—soulless. Certainly no one with a conscience would use a homemade gas chamber. Dean shuddered at the thought of the victims' terrifying and painful last minutes. His body was stiff with rage and fear that it was already too late for Stacey.

"I want to go home."

"First tell me where Stacey Bailey is. Then you can go," he promised. Go where, he hadn't specified. It wasn't a lie—not completely. What Clayton Brady chose to believe from his words was his problem.

"I don't know no Stacey."

"No, of course you wouldn't know her by her name. I doubt you knew any of them by their names. Let me educate you." He opened a file and pushed photos of Highway Dumper's victims toward him, the ones that showed them full of life. "Carolyn Harper." Dean tapped one picture. "Dylan Jenkins, Destiny Close, Jane Peterson, Angel Bellman, Eloise Granger." Each name was followed by a photo. He pushed the photo they'd borrowed from Megan of Stacey, her green eyes sparkling in the sun. "Stacey Bailey."

Sweat glistened on Clayton's forehead. "I've never seen her before. Now can I go home? I want to go home. I like my home. Mother says I can't leave it. She won't be happy that I'm not there."

Dean frowned. He jabbed at the photo of Stacey with his forefinger. "Where is she?"

"I don't know," Clayton wailed, jerking his body trying to extradite himself from his binds. "Please let me go home."

"You're not going anywhere, Brady. You killed these women. Each of them wanted to go home. Did you let them?"

"I was only doing as Mother asked. Mother always locked me away. Told me I was a bad boy. Those girls were bad. I was only doing what Mother thought best."

Dean shifted in his seat. He didn't want to be in here interviewing Clayton. He wanted to be out there, actively looking for Stacey. All available uniforms were combing the man's property in search of more bodies and had already found one grave. On further inspection, they'd identified the bones of a female in her late sixties as Juliet Brady, Clayton's mother, and he'd been told by Doctor Stone after a brief examination that the woman had died a natural death. According to medical files, she'd been dying of cervical cancer when she decided to retire to her home to live out her days, her son obligingly taking care of her. He fed, bathed, and clothed her right up until the end.

Clayton had spent the time waiting for Dean talking. He'd regaled poor Cade Watson with a story that had truly shocked and sickened him. Upon arriving at the LAC, Dean had been required to listen to the tape made and even he, who had seen and heard things that would give the average person nightmares for the rest of their lives, had been disgusted. Sitting here now with Clayton, he could understand how easily it had been to change the mind of an innocent child into a depraved and sadistic killer.

Dean could only imagine the mind-games and brutal torture she had forced upon him. By all accounts, Juliet Brady had not been the friendly, church-going woman she projected to the world. Her own dark past showed she'd been abused both physically and sexually by her father. She'd also been extremely strict on her son. The knowledge that one day he would become a man was too much for her to bear, so she'd beaten him down, breaking bones and molesting him, making him want nothing—nobody else but her.

She'd even marred his face, burning it with bleach in one of the cleansing baths Clayton had described, obviously in an effort to keep him with her. She was to be his everything: mother, lover, and provider. Dean was sick just thinking about it. There was also a rumour that Clayton's own father had also been his grandfather.

But right now Dean wasn't interested in the how and why, the excuses as to why he'd killed all those innocent women who'd never done a single thing to him. He wasn't feeling particularly understanding.

"Don't play games with me, Brady," he warned. "I'll see to it you never see daylight again. Now where is Stacey?"

Clayton's gaze moved to the photos on the table. He took a good look at the first six photos fanned across the table like a deck of cards, a small half-smile appearing on his face. Dean could see the joy in his eyes, could almost feel the sickening pleasure he got from their deaths and knew he was reliving their last moments.

Dean slammed his hand down on the table in front him, earning a jolt from the man across from him. "Stacey Bailey," he ground out through clenched teeth.

Again, Clayton looked down at the last picture and Dean had the urge to cover Stacey's sweet face from the man's murdering eyes. The need to protect her was strong.

"Pretty," Clayton said after studying the photo for some time. His fingers twitched and Dean knew he wanted to stroke the picture. "But I've never seen her before in my life. She seems like such a sweet girl. Not like the others," Clayton snarled. He glanced over at Dean. "How did you find me, Detective?"

"You made a mistake."

Clayton's expression was a mixture of intrigue and excitement, like it was all just a game. "Really, what was that?"

"Murdering six women."

Spittle landed on the table. "Those women were nothing!"

"You're wrong. They didn't deserve to die. No one has the right to take another life. No one."

Clayton smirked. "How many have you claimed? You're just like me, Detective. We've both taken lives. Both killed."

"I am nothing like you, Brady. Nothing," he said, disgusted at the very idea.

He may have killed in the past, even gotten pleasure at exacting revenge on the men who'd murdered his friends, but he would never be like Clayton Brady.

He turned on his heel and left him to his fate. As far as Dean was concerned, the man no longer existed.

Chapter 36

"He didn't take her," Natalie said as soon as Dean opened the door to the observation room located beside the interrogation room. She'd been observing the interview through the two-way mirror.

He had expected to see Nick, but Natalie was alone in the room. There was no way he could escape her, no one he could dump her on. It wasn't that he didn't like Natalie, he just didn't like psychologists as a whole. He let out a deep breath.

"No. I've already come to that conclusion. Someone out there has been using the Highway Dumper as a scapegoat."

"I agree. Brady is extremely proud of what he's done. If he took Stacey, he would be gloating as he'd done the others. I think in one way he understands they're individuals and in another believes he's enacting revenge on his mother."

"A piece of work, that one. Was it any wonder he turned out to be so twisted? But this doesn't help us. Stacey is still missing."

"It's not your fault, Dean."

"I promised her."

The door to the observation room opened and Nick entered, Maddie squirming in his arms. Dean raised an eyebrow enquiringly.

"Sorry. Natalie wanted to be present, and Maddie shouldn't be hearing anything except the Wiggles right now," he said by way of explanation. The little girl was also an expert in getting her own way. He would've thought Nick, who as far as Dean understood had a couple of nieces, would be immune to such attention seeking ways. Apparently not. He frowned. What hope did he have?

Nick placed Maddie down and she immediately latched onto Dean's leg. Not that he minded. He loved the little imp like crazy. Because of her, he knew there were still good things in this world. Not to mention the weight of her in his arms made his heart ache and brought out all his protective instincts. There were only two women he felt that way about. Dean looked down at her and she smiled, melting his heart.

"Goddamned heartbreaker," he muttered as he scooped Maddie up, holding her close. "She's going to be trouble, you know that, right?"

Natalie nodded, smiling serenely. "Oh yes, Matt and I are already preparing ourselves for that eventuality."

"Dean," Nick said, his voice serious. He glanced over at his partner and saw the hardness on his face. Dread seeped into his bones. He handed Maddie to her mother. "There's something you need to see."

Chapter 37

Nick stared across the stainless steel interrogation table at Professor Todd. The man was sweating through the silk shirt that accompanied another impeccably tailored suit. He was scared. Dean could almost smell it on the man. Fear always had a particular fruity scent, easily identifiable after you had the training. Nick looked beyond the professor to where Dean stood, leaning against the gun-metal grey walls. He nodded.

"Why am I here?" Todd asked. His voice was full of displeasure at being hauled down to the LAC.

After they'd left Natalie and Maddie, Nick had told him that he'd been delving into the professor's life after the first meeting, not entirely satisfied with his responses and Dean was grateful he had. It had taken time but Nick finally got results.

"Besides the fact that you lied to us?" Nick replied.

Dean straightened away from the wall and met the professor's gaze in the mirror on the other side of the room. He was trying to keep calm but his control was slipping. It would only take a slight push and he'd collapse.

"I never lied."

"No? Where is Stacey, Professor Todd?" Nick demanded.

"I have no idea. I wish I did."

Dean stared at the man. "Why?"

Todd frowned, seemingly confused. "Why? She's the brightest pupil in my class. Of all the classes I have taught, no one has ever shown as much potential as Stacey." He smiled as if he'd had a hand in who Stacey was becoming. "Any teacher would be proud to guide her, to shape and mould her brilliant mind."

Nausea unsettled his stomach. "And I suppose guide her right into your bedroom?"

Shock crossed his face. "Such student and teacher relations are deemed inappropriate at this school."

"And the last five schools you've taught at?" Nick retorted.

Dean's skin crawled as he stared at the man who'd caused such pain. From the moment they'd started investigating his virtual life, they'd found things that made even him, a seasoned detective, sick to his stomach. But Dean knew there was no one decent out there who could stomach the things Todd had done.

The professor glared at Nick. "Those cases were all dismissed."

"And so were you. You were lucky enough to get the job here, although as of today, you are no longer employed with the university."

"I think this interview is over," Todd said, standing huffily.

Dean pushed him back into the chair with more force than required and was slightly satisfied when Todd rubbed at his bruised shoulder. It was certainly a start.

"No, I think we're just beginning," Nick continued. "You finally went one step too far."

"I would never hurt Stacey!"

Nick shrugged. "Why not? You roughed her up." He opened a manila folder and pushed it in front of the professor. A picture of a young girl of about fifteen was stapled to the file, her body badly beaten. "Mandy Higgins, remember her? Seventeen stitches?"

He pushed aside the folder and stared stonily at him.

"Or how about these?" Nick opened four more folders and spread them out on the table. "Each of these girls trusted you as their teacher and you abused that trust."

Jason Todd crossed his arms over his chest, no longer the affable man who'd been so eager to help them days earlier in his office. "I would never hurt Stacey. I loved her."

"But Stacey didn't love you, is that it?" Dean hovered over the professor's shoulders, hoping to disconcert him.

"Stacey didn't know what she wanted," Todd said, his neck twisted so he could look at Dean. He turned back to Nick. "She needed to be loved. Her mother pushed her too far, worked her to the bone.

She needed a father figure."

Nick's face turned to stone. "So you played daddy, is that it? Guided her just like you said? What did you do to her?"

"Nothing, I swear! I'm innocent," Todd proclaimed, the perspiration that had beaded on his forehead started to run down his face. "Stacey was naïve. That's what I liked about her. She'd been kept in a suburban bubble all her life, waiting for someone to bring her to life. But I never touched her."

Nick fought to control his anger, the cords in his neck straining from the force, the faces of his four sisters most likely bouncing around his head. Nick was very protective of the fairer sex for obvious reasons. He slammed his fist on the table. "You sick son of a bitch! How'd it go down? You took a pass at her and she denied you, so you took her and had her hidden somewhere for your pleasure? What have you done to Stacey?"

"Nothing, I swear. I haven't hurt her. I didn't take her and I didn't touch her."

Nick's face was red, the vein in his temple pulsating in anger. "If she dies, you will spend the rest of your life in prison. All twenty minutes of it. You see, murderers and lifers don't like molesters, rapists, or paedophiles and believe me they *will* know what you have done."

Dean had to hand it to Nick, he was doing a fine job of being scary. Not that he hadn't said anything that wasn't true. He'd asked to do the interrogation, had cited his reasons that Dean might not be able to control himself and might accidentally kill the professor. He had conceded knowing that anything was possible and right now he was much too close to the case to be objective, might even ignore a deal offered because he wanted to rip the man's throat out. But it seemed he wasn't the only one affected by Stacey's abduction.

"I may have used those girls and I wanted Stacey, but I didn't hurt her, I swear to God." His tone pleaded for them to believe.

"So what were your plans with Stacey?" Dean asked, knowing the answer would probably only serve to anger him.

Todd leaned back in his chair and let out a deep relenting breath, knowing he was beat.

"Graduation night, I was going to offer her the world. She's a special woman, Detective. You may not know what it's like to see such potential, but I do. Stacey was going places. She is going to be the toast of the town one day, I guarantee it. Offers will be rolling in."

Nick stared at him for a moment. "So you were going to ride the money train when it came in, is that it?"

Todd's eyes shot daggers at Nick. "There is nothing wrong with that."

"Morally, yes there is."

"In the olden days, women married men all the time for money and security, so why should men be any different in modern times?"

Whoever had taken Stacey had probably saved her from Jason Todd. She could've easily ended up like his other victims. There was no way a sweet girl like Stacey would've survived Todd's sexual perversions, despite his claim to caring for her. Once a man got a taste for blood...

"I'll let you think about that for the next twenty to thirty years," Nick told him. "And if I find out you've lied to us again..."

"I'm not lying. But if you want to know who might've taken Stacey other than that killer, take a look at the student body. Uni is very competitive these days."

Dean raised an eyebrow. "Anyone in particular you have in mind?"

"Yeah. Jesse Copeland as in *the* Copelands. Harbour Bay's royalty. The man has a vindictive streak and his daddy puts a lot of pressure on him to succeed, but Jesse doesn't have it in him."

Nick closed the door firmly behind them as they stepped out. "What a piece of work."

"Yeah, but I believe him. He didn't take Stacey. His plans for her couldn't be accomplished with her in captivity, at least not all of them. We're running out of suspects." He ran his stiff fingers over his head. Jason Todd was a sexual sadist who liked beating up young, defenceless women but keeping a woman captive was harder than it sounded. It required planning, dedication, and patience. He leaned against the wall beside a bulletin board.

He was bone weary. It had been a long day that had started at the crack of dawn and the end wasn't in sight.

Matt had called earlier, before he and Nick had begun the interview with Todd, and told him that Lucy Webber was doing just fine. She'd been admitted with dehydration and minor lacerations to her fingers but she'd soon recover. Her mental health was more worrisome and Matt had already talked her into meeting with Natalie to discuss her experience. He wished her luck, and was glad he'd been there to help her. No one deserved to die at another's hand. It was why he did what he did.

He just wished he could help Stacey. Megan's face flashed through his mind. He should call her. Soon it'd be all over the news and he'd not be able to contain it. But he wanted to hold off for as long as possible. It was cowardly of him, but he needed the time to gather his courage and face her. No matter what she said, he had failed her and that thought alone was powerful enough to crush him.

He pushed away from the wall. "Arrest the son-of-a-bitch. He's not going free to hurt another woman while I'm breathing."

"I agree. Then let's go find Copeland and hopefully bring Stacey home."

Chapter 38

Dean found Jesse Copeland in the school library with a stack of textbooks in front of him, several opened to a page that he kept referring to. Nick reached the table first, drawing his attention. From the complete lack of interest he showed, Dean was sure this was not the Copeland boy's first time dealing with cops. Dean flashed his I.D. and badge, introducing both himself and Nick to the kid Professor Todd had called 'Harbour Bay Royalty.' The richest family in Harbour Bay besides the Bennetts, local shipping magnates whose leader had his fair share of underhand dealings.

The Copelands owned several hotels, their main base in Harbour Bay, and besides Jesse, had two wayward daughters who from the age of fourteen had been snapped doing everything from clubbing, drinking alcohol while underage, snorting up cocaine, and caught with their pants down in the literal sense. Jesse appeared to be the less troubled child.

He leaned back in his chair and regarded the

detectives, a slight fuzz growing on his face. Copeland was a good looking young man, the type teenage girls swooned over, which to Dean meant the slightly feminine looking male whose beauty supplies often rivalled that of a middle-aged woman. Jesse was dressed in worn jeans and a Metallica T-shirt, looking like the opposite of a rich boy, which he supposed was the idea. Something unidentifiable was smeared down the front of the shirt and from the **'no eating'** signs hanging on the walls, his food had obviously been smuggled in.

"I guess you're here to talk about Stacey," he said insolently.

Nick sat down on the desk. "Now why would you say that?"

Copeland smiled, one side of his mouth rising higher than the other. "Because I haven't done anything lately to warrant a visit from the cops. I've been keeping my nose clean, studying, you know. Got finals coming up. What else would you want to talk about except for what everyone else is talking about, which is Stacey, and I've got several classes with her. I made an assumption. Tell me I'm wrong."

Nick smiled as if he was amused, but it was more teeth than sincerity. "No, you're right, Copeland. That's why we're here."

"Am I going to need a lawyer?"

Dean narrowed his eyes. The moment a lawyer was called in, the whole show was over. That's why he hated dealing with the rich. They believed the world to be their playing ground and everyone else be damned.

252

"That depends, Copeland. Did you do anything that would require one?"

Jesse studied them for a moment, probably trying to decide whether or not they were bullshitting him. "Look, I had no beef with Stacey no matter what that ponce Professor Todd said. Sure, my old man wants me to be top of my class, but shit happens, you know? It's not like Stacey didn't deserve that title. I've committed enough of my time to being a good son. I'm not going to do it anymore and I'm certainly not going to kill for that title no matter how disappointed my father might be. I'm not going to ruin my life over something that in all hindsight no one gives a shit about."

Just how honest was Jesse being? He was a pretty good human lie detector or a bullshit monitor, always knowing if someone was trying to pull a fast one, and while he knew Jesse Copeland was as slippery as an eel, he had no doubts about the kid's sincerity.

Nick wasn't as convinced. "Not even when daddy calls the shots?"

Jesse let out a puff of breath. "Shit, man, 'Daddy' would've married me off to her before you could say *I do* if he could've. If he can't have a brain for a son, he'll have one for his son's wife. Look, nobody knows Stacey. None of us noticed her, especially not in a class our size, and she never tried to get to know us and frankly neither did we. Maybe we were a little intimidated by her."

Dean was surprised. He had expected the worst from a kid with the Copeland last name, but Jesse seemed to be a straight arrow. He'd had a few run-ins over the years—drunk driving, possession, and driving without a licence—but it appeared he wanted to make something more of his life and not just be known as a Copeland or a screw-up.

"She shot you down?" Nick asked.

Jesse snorted. A smile came to his lips and he took another moment, lost in his memories. "Hell, man, I didn't bother trying. You take one look at her and just see the stay away signs. I hope you find the man you're looking for, because Stacey didn't deserve this. What?" he asked as they stared at him. "I'm not the arsehole everybody thinks I am."

"Got any ideas as to who might've had it in for Stacey?"

The kid shook his head. "No, sorry, guys. Stacey wasn't on a lot of people's radar. 'Course, all that's changed now."

Nick thanked him for his time and the kid shook each of their hands before stuffing his head back into the nearest book.

They stepped away, unconsciously moving without making any noise as they headed past the stacks containing the books on social science and towards the exit.

"Great, so we're back to square one with no viable suspects. The kid who was supposed to have a seething grudge against Stacey doesn't, so who does that leave?"

Chapter 39

Dean leaned heavily against the wall of the conference centre, feeling more desperate than before. The longer Stacey was out there, the more dangerous it was for her. He couldn't help but feel as if time was running out for her.

"The professor is a sexual deviant, but my gut says he had nothing to do with Stacey's abduction. Same goes for the Copeland kid." He tucked his hands into his trouser pockets. "We checked with the admissions office, and no one else was on par with her academically in the same field. We reinterviewed the teachers and none know of any hostility against Stacey. I'm at a loss on what to do next." He hated admitting that out loud.

Once again, they were starting from the beginning, but this time had less information to go on than before. He'd yet to call Megan, putting off the inevitable for as long as possible. He wasn't ready to hear the disappointment and anger in her voice just yet, knowing he was probably causing more problems between them the longer he kept her in the dark.

"What about Megan Bailey?" Darryl asked.

He frowned. "What about her?"

"What if it's not about Stacey at all, but Megan? She is the more visible one and according to Nick, they could be twins. What if we're looking at a case of mistaken identity?"

Dean ran a hand over his head. He didn't like the fact that the idea had merit. He'd like to veto the suggestion right then and there, but he couldn't. It was a possibility and if they didn't find something soon that would lead them on a path to Stacey's kidnapper, they'd have to analyse that line of rational thought more closely.

A whisper of memory floated across his mind. He pushed away from the wall. He couldn't believe he hadn't seen it before. He'd been too distracted by Megan to think straight.

"Megan receives threats on a weekly basis. Unhappy readers and over-enthusiastic fans. She mentioned one was particularly disturbing."

Matt's eyebrow rose. "Was it ever investigated?"

He wished he knew. He hadn't thought to ask the question. "I'm not sure. Riley, Megan's editor, has copies."

"Let's look into them. Meanwhile, I'm going to do an in-depth search on both Baileys. See if we can't dig up some skeletons."

While the team disbanded, Dean dialled Megan's number, frowning when her voicemail picked up the call. He couldn't blame her for not answering. His behaviour had been appalling. However, they were dealing with an open case and he needed to talk to her.

Nick stopped beside him. "Megan not answering?"

He exhaled deeply raggedly. Her presence had been a balm to his wounded soul, and now she was gone.

"I know I seriously fucked up. But dammit, we need to talk."

Nick's eyebrow rose.

"Yeah, I know," he continued, before Nick could say a word. "Being pissy isn't going to help matters. Would you mind heading over to her place and filling her in? Stay with her until all this is sorted. I don't want her alone right now."

"You must be really be concerned if you're actually asking me to hang out with her."

"Yeah, well, I'm guessing she wouldn't be too happy to see me right now."

He saw compassion in his partner's eyes before the man left to do his bidding. Soon, he'd talk to Megan, but for now…someone else would be able to help him.

Chapter 40

Dean knocked on the open door to Riley O'Neill's office. Her head jerked up at the sound and she flashed him a dazzling smile. She stood and came around her desk wearing a charcoal skirt suit that covered her petite body demurely and three-inch black heels. He studied her face now that Megan wasn't around to distract him. She was beautiful with a creamy complexion and her eyes were a brilliant blue, like the deepest part of the ocean. Pretty. Just not for him.

"Detective Matthews. To what do I owe this pleasure?"

He relaxed slightly. For a moment he'd wondered if Megan had complained to her friend over his behaviour. She had the right to, after the way he'd treated her. But it would make things more expedient if Riley was willing.

"I'd like your help."

"Of course. Come in."

He moved further into her office. It was a far cry from his own. For starters, she had walls and a nice view. It was also spacious with expensive furniture and a sleek, professional look. He had a scarred desk, out of date equipment, and a chair without proper back support. "The night we met, you mentioned Megan had received threats."

"Meredith," she said. "To the public, there is no Megan, only Meredith. It's an important distinction to remember. Why are you interested? They're harmless, I assure you."

He settled his gaze on hers. "We're taking a different direction in the investigation."

She frowned. "Why?"

"We caught the Highway Dumper today."

Riley's eyes immediately filled with tears. "Stacey?"

"Was never his victim."

Riley closed her eyes for a moment and took an unsteady breath. When she reopened them, they were clear. Dean respected the hell out of her. She reminded him of Megan. It was probably what made them such good friends and it was clear Riley cared a great deal about her cousin.

"I'm not sure if that's good news or bad. So you believe what exactly?" She folded her arms across her chest. "That one of Meredith's crazed fans is responsible?"

"It's a possibility."

"One that has merit. But I told you. They're harmless."

He accepted her analysis but would rather make his own assessment. He was trained for this, and she was not.

"You receive all correspondence?"

"Yes."

"I'd like to see them all. Especially the one Megan spoke of that night. She seemed to be particularly scared of it."

"I know the one. It was delivered directly to Meg's apartment. It freaked the crap out of her and for good reason. It was vile."

"Her apartment? So someone knew she was Meredith Baker?" he asked, feeling the tendrils of anticipation curl inside him.

"Yes. But it's not what you're looking for," she replied as if reading his mind.

"May I have it?" he asked, ignoring her adamant response. Not that he didn't respect Riley's opinion, but this was about Stacey and Megan and he wasn't leaving anything to chance.

Riley bit her lower lip. "I don't have it anymore."

Dean felt like he was going to explode; so close, yet so far. He turned his back to her and stared out the window at the skyline as he took calming breaths. He clenched his jaw in an effort to control the anger bubbling beneath the surface.

"Relax. I didn't throw it out or destroy it or whatever stupid thing you think I've done. Give me some credit."

He glanced at her reflection on the glass in time to see her roll her eyes. Despite the situation, he smiled. She looked so annoyed and damn cute at the same time. He doubted she would appreciate his thoughts.

"I take all threats to my writers seriously, Detective, and have them all looked at by a trained professional who chases any that pose a serious concern."

Dean crossed his arms over his chest and turned to look down at her. "And who is this trained professional?" Scepticism coated his tone.

"My brother. He's a senior constable and works in a special taskforce in Melbourne. Don't ask me which one, he's not big on the details. But he does know how to weed out the crazies and I figured he would have contacts that could do all sorts of things that maybe you normal guys couldn't."

"And what did he find?"

She sat on the edge of her desk and regarded him. "Like I said, nothing that can help. He traced the letter back to the writer. The thing is, it came back to Cathy Bailey, Megan's aunt. I didn't have the heart to tell her someone related to her could be so cold and callous. Megan and Stacey mean the world to me. I'd do anything not to have them hurt. Cathy may be a vicious bitch, but they're just words. If I thought she'd act on them, I'd have her arrested."

Dean found himself surprised. He wasn't entirely sure why it should surprise him, as Cathy Bailey had been extremely against Megan's chosen profession, but he didn't believe she would actually harm either of the women. As far as he could tell, she was all talk—and more talk but no action. Even now, her daughter was missing for days, and she still hadn't shown up in town.

"You're going to bring Stacey home safely, aren't you?" Riley asked, her eyes pleading and vulnerable. It was like a knife to his heart.

"I'm going to try my best, Ms. O'Neill."

Riley studied him shrewdly. "Megan told me what you promised her. Such a foolish thing to do, Detective. But I know it comes from a good place. I just want a happy ending for Megan, you know. She needs Stacey to come home. I need her to come home." Her face hardened. "Break her heart and I'll break you."

Dean stared down at her. Riley was several inches shorter than him and petite in size. A stiff wind would snap her like a twig. Had the warning come from another woman he would have waved it off, but underneath those red curls he knew she could back up her threat.

"I'll find Stacey."

"That's not what I was talking about and you know it."

He bowed his head. "Your threat has been noted."

Chapter 41

Dean raged, knocking the file folders from his desk and thumped his fist against the wall. Pain, sharp and intense, plunged deep with a final gut-wrenching twist. Tears blurred his vision and his heart missed a beat. For a second, he'd thought it was the end. It might as well have been. He banged his fist against the wall again and again until the skin broke and blood ran free. Plaster embedded itself into the wound but he didn't really notice, didn't feel anything anymore, numb from the knowledge that Megan had been taken.

Natalie grabbed hold of him painfully, hard enough so he would focus on her, hard enough to bruise. Where did this strength come from? Where had she come from? He'd not seen her since the interview with Clayton, but it was clear she hadn't left. He really wished she had. He wanted no witnesses to his meltdown.

"Just breathe in and out." Her calming voice penetrated the haze. His throat worked as he imagined a range of tortures Megan was enduring, and that was the worst torment he could imagine for himself.

Dean shot her a look. As if breathing would help anyone. Not breathing, however, had possibilities. His eyes continued to fill with unshed tears and he was ashamed of them, looking away from Natalie to focus on the smallest pinprick of a hole on the wall. Years ago, it had been filled with a nail, and now it had been removed and was left empty—just like him. Megan brought so much light into his life. Smiling or laughing hadn't be a daily thing before he'd met her. Now he hardly recognised the man he had been, so dark and gloomy, the quintessential brooding male.

Natalie rubbed her hands up and down his arms. "Relax, Dean."

How could he relax? He'd failed both Megan and Stacey. Now they were in the hands of an unknown man, and they didn't know his motives. Was it sexual? Manipulative? Sadistic? The list went on and on. The trouble with being a cop was that he knew exactly what lurked beyond doors and behind corners, had seen the most horrible things imaginable and then some. It was hard to remain positive or believe the best in people.

He clenched his hands into fists again, feeling the sharp pinch of the plaster that had lodged itself into his hand. The urge to hit something was strong, almost overpowering his other senses, preferably the man who held the woman he—

Dean let out a deep, shaky breath.

Natalie raised an eyebrow when she saw his hands. She wasn't afraid, despite her past—the victim of an abusive stepfather. She knew Dean would never hurt her, couldn't even if he wanted to. It wasn't the type of man he was. But he was still amazed at her level of trust in him.

"You love her, Dean," Natalie said softly. "And I know that's hard to accept especially for you. But trust me, loving the right person puts all your fears to rest."

Dean glared at her for over-stepping her bounds. He hated when she became Doctor Murphy.

She smiled sadly. "I'm sorry I can't help but read you, and since Megan came onto the scene, you've been sending out distress signals like a man drowning. You're not in a war zone anymore, Dean. I'm not going to lie and say I know what you're going through. It had to have been awful to have such a lasting impression on you, and I'm not going to say I'll try to understand because I know I won't be able to."

He didn't want to think or feel, never wanted to be in the position to let someone down—someone counting on him. "I promised myself I would never allow myself to get into this position. Feeling, caring, loving…it's all for the weak, the vulnerable. I wanted no part of it."

He noticed his rage moved over her without issue.

"I know you care about her and that scares you." Holding his gaze, Natalie didn't allow him to break away. "You've been alone for so long you don't know how to deal with something so strong. You're in love with her, aren't you? Admit it."

Dean stubbornly stood there, his jaw clenched.

Camille Taylor

Natalie raised an eyebrow, crossing her arms across her chest while she patiently waited him out.

Letting out another deep breath, his mind went inward as he relived the past few days. Meeting Megan, her gorgeous eyes filled with worry. The powerful reaction he had to her. Her smile, the way she loved him. Megan lying beneath him as he moved above her. He let out a cry, one filled with anguish.

He sank down in his chair and buried his face in his hands. "Dammit, I am." He glared up at her. "And you, Doctor Natalie, are a pain in my arse."

She grinned at him. Doctor Murphy was always reserved for when he was being professional. Doctor Natalie was when he was being sarcastic, and just Natalie when she was a friend and the wife of a co-worker.

She became serious again. "Don't think about Megan right now or Stacey. She should be nothing but a victim in your mind and you are a great detective. Don't forget that."

"I never wanted to deal with any of this. I promised myself I would never get involved, never care about someone so much it hurt."

He looked up and found his entire team and one toddler staring at him in empathy.

Matt inclined his head. "Welcome to the club. Your life will never be the same."

Natalie playfully hit Matt on his shoulder. "Don't tell him that. You'll scare him even more."

Matt wrapped his free arm around his wife's waist and pulled her towards him, into the comfort and safety of his arms. These two were obviously in love with each other, a beautiful daughter who was the product of that love resting on her father's hip and reaching out towards her mother. It hit him hard in the chest. Dean wanted that too. All he had to do was get his woman back. Failure was not an option because as much as he didn't want to be the man who loved someone so much he couldn't live without the other person, he knew with Megan gone he had no reason to continue.

Dean swiped his hand over his head. "No. It's all right. I'm finally getting it. Now let's get to work. We have some women to find."

Natalie took Maddie from Matt's arms as they all moved into their professional modes. Matt, Darryl, James, Dean, and Nick all put on their cop faces, as they once again ran through the facts of the case. But working with absolute certainly that Stacey's disappearance had no correlation to the Highway Dumper made it easier.

Dean closed his eyes at the thought of some creep's hands on Megan's body, but trusted her not to allow him to hurt her. She would only allow the sick fuck so much before she struck back. Megan was no wallflower and was probably analysing the situation now.

Hold on, baby. I'm coming. Dean opened his eyes, his team filling his vision. *We're coming.* It was great to be a part of the team, of the Harbour Bay family.

"So...tell us," Darryl ordered as he leaned against his desk, arms crossed.

Dean's heart ached with pain for a brief moment until he composed himself. This was not a time for

Dean, Megan's lover. It was time for Dean, Detective Senior Sergeant and former army infantryman. He detailed what Nick had told him, that upon arriving at Megan's apartment he'd found the place empty. When she couldn't be located, they started a city wide manhunt which led to the parking lot at Tanner's. She was a fighter and wouldn't have gone down easy. He only hoped she'd gotten in a couple good shots.

"Okay, this is where we need to get creative, men." Matt cleaned off the whiteboard. "This joker has been one step ahead of us this whole time, using the Highway Dumper to get away with kidnapping two women. So what do we know, and who do we suspect?"

Dean told them about Cathy Bailey and her threatening note, Professor Todd and his disturbing interest in Stacey, and then stopped short, suddenly realising that was all he had in the way of suspects.

James joined in. "If Cathy Bailey wanted Megan out of the picture, why not just kill her? Why the elaborate kidnapping?"

They ignored the tightening of Dean's muscles and the look of pure rage that was sure to be on his face as they spoke so casually about Megan's death. He knew they meant nothing by it, but the thought of her death hit him where it hurt.

"I've run through those connected with Stacey and Megan." Matt quickly replaced the blank whiteboard with names. "For quiet people, they have some sickos on the fringes of their lives and some interesting characters too. For instance, Megan's editor, Riley Siobhan O'Neill is the daughter of a decorated cop and her brother works for the SOG in Melbourne."

Dean's eyebrow rose. SOG was the Special Operations Group, men trained in tactical warfare who were called in for high risk situations. That certainly explained some things. Riley was no pushover.

"Something to be aware of...she has a registered gun and apparently knows how to use it."

Dean's mouth twitched despite the circumstances. Why wasn't he surprised? It made her threat more credible. Not that he had to worry, because he had no plans to hurt Megan. The man who took her was another matter.

"Stacey was an accident," Natalie said. "I don't think we're dealing with a killer, otherwise we would've already have found Stacey's body. Although there's no telling what the kidnapper plans to do now that the real object of his obsession is in his grasp."

"You have no idea who would want to harm her?" James's gaze found his.

Dean shook his head sadly.

"I don't believe it's about harming her." Natalie turned so she could see each man. "Yes, she got hate mail, but I'm betting she also got letters from adoring fans too. Megan is a public figure. Her books are in homes all across the country and whether she acknowledges it or not, pieces of her inner thoughts. It's not a stretch to think someone created a fantasy out of it, thinking her books were speaking directly to them. That they're a special portal, connecting him to her."

"He would've had to meet her in person to keep the reality alive in his mind," Matt said. "She never mentioned any male fans who were overly enthusiastic? Besides Nick," he added wryly.

Nick flipped him off.

"No, but when we get her back, I'll be sure to ask her about every man she's ever met, okay?" Dean said angrily. He knew Matt was only trying to help but his questions only served to point out how useless he was.

Natalie cleared her throat. "As much as I think you'd love that," she began, shifting Maddie on her hip, "I doubt she would remember him, even if he'd been standing right in front of her. He probably didn't even register on her radar, but she registered on his."

Great. If it was an over-eager fan, that covered a lot of area. Why the hell did Megan have to be so damn good at what she did? He ran his hand over his face to drive away the weariness. "I wouldn't even know where to start looking," he said, exasperated. "It could be anyone in the country."

"He has to be in town. Somewhere close enough for him to keep tabs on her."

Natalie was right, but...

"But Megan doesn't go anywhere except B&G."

Her eyes lit up. Enthusiastically, she said, "There you go. You went from having a country full of suspects to a town and finally down to a building. He won't hurt her, Dean. That's not what he wants."

"And we all know how easy it is for these creeps to build up a relationship with someone they hardly know. You see it all the time with stalkers believing they belong with the other person who they'd never met," Nick said.

Natalie shook her head. "No, this goes beyond seeing and wanting. He's built a life surrounded by her. He'd know everything about her and I wouldn't be surprised if you find his fingerprints inside her apartment. He's been there, I guarantee it."

"We're already running all the fingerprints Forensics pulled from Megan's car. I also checked with Tanner. None of his CCTV cameras pointed towards the section where Megan had parked. I'm sorry, Dean," Nick said, guilt lacing his voice.

"It's not your fault. It would've happened anyway. Whoever this is, he's very determined." It wasn't Nick's fault and he hated to think of him being in pain because of it. He was a good guy, an honourable man. He shouldn't be blaming himself.

If anyone was to blame, it was Dean. If he hadn't acted like an arse, Megan wouldn't have been at Tanner's alone.

"I doubt he'll be in the system," Natalie said. "He's led an uneventful life so far. He lives in fantasy, not reality. To feed such an obsession I'd say he's been on the cusp of her life for some time now—watching, waiting—and since the publishing house is Megan's one constant, I'd suggest you start there."

Dean nodded. "I'll get Riley to give me a list of every man who works at B&G, including other authors."

And with any luck, one might be their guy.

Chapter 42

Riley looked up from her desk as a large body invaded her office. She studied Detective Matthews's face, and something in those tormented eyes had her lungs expanding, robbing her of breath. Pain, fresh and raw, screamed out from every pore. Her own feelings were mirrored in him. He didn't bother with useless formalities, cutting straight to the point.

"I need a list of every man in this building including the mailman, Ms. O'Neill. We're working on the surmise that the person who took Megan is infatuated with her, likely obsessed."

Riley sat back in her chair, a frown tugging at her eyebrows. "Sounds like Big Shot Johnson."

"Big Shot Johnson?"

"Kenneth Johnson. He's an editor, as well, with a serious hard-on for Megan." She winced at her choice of words when his jaw tightened. "He's pissed at me. Originally, Megan's manuscript was on his desk, but Johnson thinks he's too good to read unsolicited mail, so I took over that job. Which was how I discovered Megan. He recently offered his services to her, but she turned him down."

"Where's his office?"

Her eyes widened at Dean's tone. She hadn't truly believed Johnson to be a suspect, but Dean sure did from the serious glower on his face. She stood, slipping her feet into her three-inch stilettos. He followed her down a hall, then another, before she stopped outside a heavy wooden oak door. She turned the knob, but Dean stopped her before pushing the door wide open. She followed him into the room and noticed for the first time that his gun was drawn as he quickly cleared the room.

Her heartbeat thundered in her chest. Not because of the gun. She'd been raised in a household full of weapons—even owned her own. The seriousness Dean took to her suggestion about Johnson worried her. Had he really had something to do with Megan's disappearance?

She swallowed hard as Dean holstered the gun. He moved over to Johnson's desk to flip through the paperwork lying about.

"Surely you don't think he'd be stupid enough to have his kidnapping plan advertised on his desk?" Her body trembled and she was afraid her knees might give out at any moment.

"Actually, I am. People spend most of their lives in their offices these days. You'd be surprised what they leave about."

She couldn't fault his logic. She kept her entire life on her computer—photos, contacts, and even legal documents. She would be screwed if anything happened to the hard drive.

He stared at the monitor of Johnson's computer. "Do you have the password?"

"No, but I can get IT to reset it."

"Do it," he ordered.

Riley moved closer to the desk. "Isn't that illegal? Some sort of wrongful search and seizure that could harm the court case?"

"If the guy is innocent, no harm no foul. If he's not, he's not going to trial."

The fierce expression gave weight to his words and she shivered. There was no mistaking his meaning. She wasn't frightened for her safety. His anger wasn't toward her. Nor was she worried about the man who held Stacey and Megan, because he'd get what was coming to him. She immediately picked up the handset of Johnson's phone and dialled an extension.

Within a minute they were logged on and she was navigating through the convoluted C Drive packed to the last gigabyte with data. Because of that, the computer ran frustratingly slow. Dean hovered over her shoulder and she could sense his increasing impatience. Thankfully, Johnson wasn't security conscious so they'd not encountered any password protected folders which either meant he was innocent or extremely arrogant. But then she already knew he was the latter.

She opened a folder, then another, and the computer stopped responding. Dean cursed savagely. She didn't try to soothe him. She was in agreement. Tapping her fingernails impatiently on the polished wood desk, she waited for the folder to finish loading. Hundreds of smaller files marked with a date appeared and she clicked on the first one, her mouth forming an O.

In front of them were several hundred surveillance photos, each and every one of them of Megan. "I thought he had a thing for her...professionally, I mean. This is sick. I had no idea. No wonder he always had me read the manuscripts," she said, more to herself than to Dean. "He never had the time by the looks of it. How can someone live their own lives if they're so wrapped up in someone else's?" She glanced at Dean as if expecting him to have the answer.

"Easy. He doesn't have a life, or at least won't have one when I'm done with him."

His voice was enough to make a lesser person shiver, but since Riley felt the same way she didn't flinch. She knew if she was given half the chance, she would rip Kenneth Johnson into pieces with her bare hands. She didn't even bother to mask those feelings. She wasn't about to lie to herself or anyone who asked. She wanted his head on a platter.

Behind her, she heard Dean talking on his mobile to another detective, asking for Johnson's particulars as she continued to flick through his files. The drive was badly disorganised but she was beginning to understand his particular filing system. It was only too easy to see how his work had suffered. It appeared he no longer cared about it and unfortunately it was too clear to see exactly what he *did* care about. Thousands of surveillance photos of Megan existed on the hard drive. Shots taken from afar with a long range lens, and close-ups that meant he must've been practically on top of her to take the picture. Riley shivered at the knowledge that the creep had followed her around for what seemed like months, probably even years documenting everything she did, everyone she saw. There were some things that were just plain private.

Gulping back the urge to gag, Riley continued to search the hard drive. The man had no privacy settings whatsoever on his computer. You'd think a man who spent his days spying on a woman as she went about her business would understand the need to safeguard against unauthorised viewing. But he wasn't the brightest bulb in the box. He was methodical, though. Every photo had a timestamp and location listed in the file. He appeared to document everything. She noticed several notations reading, *Megan saw the red-haired witch for lunch,* and smiled. Riley liked the idea that she pushed his buttons.

Clicking on an icon, a new file opened, showing scanned pictures of a blue-print to a house and a PDF full of décor ideas and local stock lists. She frowned as she scrolled down the pages, a feeling of familiarity overcoming her. Her mind ran through the data, matching images with what she could remember. After a few moments, it clicked.

"What is it?" Dean leaned over shoulder. She smelled the minty mouthwash on his breath.

Riley turned her head to face him. He moved back slightly. "Have you ever read any of Megan's books?"

"No. I started one, but haven't had the chance to finish."

"Well, if you had, you'd know this design here."
She tapped the computer screen showing the 2-D
image of a bedroom, complete with colour and
furniture. "This is Dahlia Blake's boudoir exactly
how Megan described it." She shook her head.
Johnson was one sick man.

"He believes this to be real, that he's Cole and
she's Dahlia." His lips thinned. "I already knew it to
be a possibility. Our resident psychologist brought
up that fact not long ago."

"I just can't believe I never saw it."

"No one wants to believe the monster next door
is anything but a normal man."

Riley nodded and exited out of the PDF, moving
along to the next large file. It took a while to
download, the file larger than the others. Her mouth
formed a grimace as the file opened and the video
began to play. There was no sound, but she instantly
felt like puking.

"Oh my God, that pervert!" Outraged, yet unable
to take her gaze from the screen, Riley tracked
Megan's movements as her friend, holding a mug in
her hands, sat down in her recliner.

A moment later, Stacey entered the family room,
backpack on her shoulder, ready for school. She
spoke with Megan for a few minutes before leaving.
Riley fast-forwarded the video, the file going for
more than a few hours. Megan's figure moved
quickly. For hours she typed, only getting up for a
refill of coffee or maybe a bathroom break. She
admired her level of concentration. No wonder she
always handed in her novels on time and complete.
The woman was almost a machine.

On screen, she stood and stretched, her shirt riding high to reveal her skin before walking out of the family room. The video continued to play for a few more minutes before clicking off and Riley, without any prompting from Dean, double-clicked another thumbnail. The camera clicked on again as Megan in tights and a tank walked into the room, the camera obviously on a motion timer. From the angle, Riley recognised the camera had to have been set up on the opposite corner of the room to Megan's recliner where the sick son-of-a-bitch could watch her for hours on end. There was rarely a time she didn't sit in that chair. Riley was outraged on Megan's behalf, and felt an overwhelming need to track Johnson down and remove something extremely precious to him.

Riley could feel Dean's breath on the back of her neck as he watched Megan begin a series of Yoga moves, her side facing the camera. Even though he wasn't touching her, she could feel the tension in his body and it was infecting the air around them, making it crackle with electricity. She felt comforted in the knowledge that he wanted to rip Johnson to shreds just as much as she did. Riley knew she could be ruthless at times, but she wasn't alone.

"Can I see that?"

Riley nodded barely a second before Dean leaned down, crowding her body and took control of the mouse. He scrolled through the file of videos and found a certain date and time—a recent one, she noted—and played the video. He fast forwarded the footage to a particular time, his eyes hard and face impassive. He clenched his jaw, his teeth snapping together. She kept her gaze on the screen, determined to see what was so fascinating to Dean. She squinted as she saw a brief movement in the corner of the screen, barely there. A hand moved into frame and then moved out, the subjects standing just outside the arch of the family room, out of the camera's range. A dark shadow moved on the wall in the room and something soft hit the ground in the centre of the arch.

**

Dean held his breath before letting it all out in one long exhale. Thankfully, the camera hadn't recorded any compromising positions between them. All of the scenes he was featured in were purely on a professional basis, yet rather frequent.

Riley frowned. "Is that…are you?" She stopped, biting on her lower lip as a blush so deep it matched her hair rose from the collar of her shirt.

"Is it noticeable?" Dean ignored her blush. He had more important things to worry about besides having an awkward conversation with her.

She shook her head. "No, but I assumed since you were particularly interested in the timestamp…"

A heavy weight lifted. "Just checking. I don't want Megan in any more danger. Perps like this see her as an object to covet. If the object doesn't want to play along, it could get bad. I only hope for Megan's sake she plays along with his sick fantasies enough to keep him happy and doesn't antagonise him."

Riley raised an eyebrow. "Are you kidding? Megan is the queen of antagonising people. You obviously never heard her speak to her annoying aunt. People think I have a temper." She shrugged, adding, "Well, I do, but still I'm not the only one."

Dean ran his fingers through his hair. "Remind me never to piss her off *or* you."

Riley answered with a bright smile. "Wise choice."

Dean regarded her for a moment. She was tiny. He could easily subdue her in a matter of seconds but she was forceful, a strong personality, and if the red hair was any indication she had one hell of a temper. He also sensed she wasn't very forgiving. It would be dangerous for anyone to cross her, but if there was anyone he'd want in his corner, it would be her. She wasn't one to back down and he sensed she'd fight until the very end. But for her all spunk, she was also soft-hearted. Sugar and spice. He wasn't entirely sure how to label Riley, but scary was a word that came to mind.

"Thanks for your assistance."

She levelled him with a look. "Just bring Meg and Stace home."

His phone rang as he stepped out of Johnson's office, moving past her assistant towards the elevator. He pulled it from his pocket and answered it.

Nick's words came clearly through the speaker. "I have an address."

Chapter 43

Megan's head throbbed. Her fingers dug into something soft. A bed. Only it wasn't her bed. The smells surrounding her fed the nausea and she tried to soothe her rebelling stomach. She took calming breaths and breathed in the scent of fresh lacquer. She slowly opened her eyes, waiting for the dizziness and swirling to stop before focusing on her surroundings.

It was not a typical bedroom. The décor and colouring was elaborate, more for aesthetics than comfort, and strangely familiar. The walls were a midnight blue complemented by ivory white curtains and duvet.

Panic overwhelmed her, threatening to pull her back under. Her heart pounded and her vision wavered. Had she gone home with someone? It wasn't like her, and although Dean wasn't her favourite person right now, she wouldn't have willingly taken up with another. The very idea was abominable. A sob caught in her throat at how they'd left it, robbing her of breath. She loved him.

There was no point in denying it.

"You look beautiful," a man said.

As she sat up, her grogginess abated, replaced by adrenaline, alertness—and fear. Oh yes, she was definitely afraid. Her memory returned, and she knew immediately that she hadn't gone home with a man willingly. The pain in her lower back told her she'd been hit with a Taser. She brought her knees up to her chin, as if that alone would protect her while she stared at the man sitting on the bed, so close to her. His spicy scent nauseated her more than the fear assaulting her.

As a person used to dealing with conflict in the pages of her books, she was widely out of her element facing the situation as Megan Bailey and not Dahlia Blake. God, how she wished she was more like her, a character that had been created from everything Megan desired in herself.

What the hell had she done to find herself in this situation and how would she get out of it? She clenched her jaw. The last thing she wanted was for Dean to have to investigate her murder. But she knew him well enough to know he'd investigate her death without the backing of the Harbour Bay LAC if he had to.

"Who are you?"

"The man of your dreams." His gaze ran over her, his voice low, almost a whisper as if they shared some mutual secret. "The man you write about in your books."

She shook her head. "He's just fiction. A made-up person. He doesn't exist."

Megan glanced around the room, assessing it like

Dean might've done. She noticed only one door, nothing she could use as a weapon. She was all alone. No Dean. No hero to save the day. Just her.

Oh boy. They were screwed. They—where *was* Stacey?

She studied the room again, noting familiar objects. She had seen this place before, but she couldn't remember when or how, the memory just out of reach. She slowly took in the room again.

Her attention snapped back when the man spoke again. "Do you like it? It's just as you asked, isn't it? The way you wanted it."

What the hell was he going on about? Her brain hadn't quite returned to its normal functioning rate. Memories bounced around her head like scenes from a movie. The research she'd done looking for the perfect house, the perfect décor and design. She suddenly gagged, her eyes going wide as she recalled where she'd seen the room before—in her dreams and imagination.

She was sitting inside Dahlia Blake's bedroom. The character from her book.

She wasn't dealing with a functioning adult here. He seemed to believe her books to be real, that she was Dahlia and he was Cole, the hunky cop in her story. Her breathing faltered and she swallowed hard.

His admiring gaze roiled her stomach. A memory suddenly popped into her head and she knew where she'd seen him before. The publishing house—he worked there with Riley and Michelle. She remembered the day at B&G when he'd offered to take her on. Big Shot Jackson, she recalled. It was him all along. He had taken Stacey because he wanted Megan. If something happened to Stacey she would never forgive herself for getting her involved. Not that she'd been a part of Johnson's decision to fixate on her, but still, a conscience wasn't always rational.

She glared at him. If she was to die, she wanted to go down scratching and biting and fighting for her life and that of her cousin who'd gone through so much. Her hand curled into a fist. If he'd hurt her—what was she talking about? Of course he'd hurt her. He'd taken her from the life she knew and held her captive. Stacey would always remember this time in her life, would have nightmares over it in the coming years, and the anger inside Megan began to burn and smoulder.

"Where is Stacey?" She added steel to her voice to show she wasn't afraid even though she was.

Johnson frowned as if he wasn't sure who she was talking about. Megan bit back the urge to hit him. Not only was she at a disadvantage, but he could easily overpower her. She didn't care what he did to her, she just needed to know where Stacey was and if she was still alive.

Oh God, please let her be alive.

"She's safe, like you are." Johnson raised his hand to stroke her cheek. Megan blocked his hand before he could touch her.

"You didn't answer my question. Where is Stacey?"

Johnson slid off the bed, turning on Megan as he paced up and down beside her. "Forget about her. This is our time." He frowned. "Why must you talk

284

about her when we're finally here together? Tell me what you think."

He moved back and forth, his eager expression waiting for an answer. He was volatile, ready to explode, his demeanour changing from delirious to angry to hopeful in a matter of seconds. What could she say? She didn't want to pull the trigger on his tightly wound brain. Whatever she said and did would greatly affect their lives, so she took a page out of her own book. If he believed himself to be Cole, she had no choice but to be Dahlia—at least until she found Stacey.

She took a steadying breath, the role an unfamiliar one. But who better to play the part of Dahlia Blake than the woman who'd created her, who'd spilled all her hidden desires into a bestselling novel?

Megan smiled as brightly as she could while seductively batting her dark lashes. "Of course I like it, why wouldn't I? After all, you went to so much effort for me." She held her breath, waiting a few excruciating seconds, wondering if Johnson was buying her act.

"It was nothing. I would do anything for you."

Megan bit her tongue to stop herself from asking about her cousin. It would be best to lead up to her, just after she got him off his guard.

"I can see that." She wasn't about to lead him on, her whole body rejecting the thought of taking it too far. So long as she could get what she wanted without tying herself up in his little drama.

"I'm so glad you're pleased. I've been so worried."

"Why didn't you just invite me here? Why kidnap me?" she asked, adding a little censure into her voice, allowing him to hear her displeasure. Maybe he would seek to placate her by taking her to Stacey, otherwise she'd have to play the game a little longer and wheedle it out of him.

His tone turned stern. "Your home is with me. I had to rescue you. You were taken from me."

Megan frowned, sure she missing something. "Taken? By whom?"

"By that girl. She took you from me, brought you to that house. If it wasn't for her we could have been together so much sooner. But it all worked out in the end, because I had time to complete this for you, for your homecoming."

His delusions were more complicated than she'd first assumed. How could he believe any of what he was saying? But of course he did, there were thousands of people out there just as disjointed with reality, and if there wasn't, her books wouldn't do nearly as well in the sales department.

She remembered the week Stacey had shown up on her doorstep. It had been a while now and she shivered in the knowledge that he'd been watching her ever since. Did he know about Dean? No, she decided. Any man who believed himself to be so in love with a woman would never have allowed another man to touch what he deemed as his. As Dean's image flashed in her mind, an inner strength blossomed inside her body. She would survive this. Just so she could see him again. As afraid as she was, Megan was more afraid of never telling him how she felt—even if her feelings weren't reciprocated. Her memory of their time together would not be tainted by their last meeting. She would hold onto those memories until she was old and grey, if she lived that long.

"It's all been an adventure, like in your books. Maybe you can write one about us. About our love." His voice brought her back to the present. She was cooler, more scared when Dean wasn't in her thoughts.

She frowned. "I write adventures. I don't live them, and if you think I'm writing about you, you have another thing coming." The words were out of her mouth before she could stop herself. The contempt she felt was coming through. She closed her eyes, mentally preparing herself for the thunder of anger. "You kidnapped my cousin, did only God knows what to her. How could you ever think I could forgive you for that?" Tears rolled down her cheeks.

It was mainly fear of the repercussions from her outburst that had the little salty drops dangling from her eyelashes. She had tried to be brave, but she had to face it, she wasn't Dahlia Blake. She couldn't lie worth a damn and was fully prepared to take the heat for it. She wished Stacey hadn't been caught up in it.

Johnson recoiled at her words before shaking his head. "Oh, no. I didn't touch her. I had to remain pure for you."

Chapter 44

Megan waited as he opened the door to what she assumed must've been his garage at one point, and turned on the light. She spotted the huddled form of Stacey in the corner, the strong scent of urine and unwashed human confined to a small space assaulting her nose. Stacey blinked at the harsh light, her arm coming up to block out the harmful rays from her sensitive eyes. Her arm quivered as she tried to hold it up but finally the weight became too much to bear and it dropped heavily to her lap. When she saw her, a mix of hope and fear appeared on Stacey's face and she shook her head slightly as if warning her.

"Oh my God, Stacey." She ran towards her cousin and dropped to her knees before Stacey and wrapped her arms around her, holding her close, letting her feel her strength and the strong beat of her pounding heart. Stacey felt so good in her arms. The fear for her cousin overrode any rational thought she might have had. Only now did her brain begin to compute the various problems she faced with explicit detail.

Before Stacey had been a dream, something she had to touch to believe, but holding her in her arms, she became real, a vulnerability to her should Johnson decide to use it. Stacey surely couldn't help her, as her body had been ravaged from lack of food and movement, exhausted from crying and the fear that would've kept her up at night. She stroked her matted hair. The girl was extremely dehydrated and scared, her wide eyes completely focused on the threat before them. Even now she could feel her delicate body shake with fear.

"See, she's all right. Now nothing can get in our way. Now we can be together forever," Johnson said, as if not seeing the torture he had inflicted.

Megan had been extremely relieved when Stacey hadn't shied away from her, hadn't lashed out at her out of fear and self-preservation. She'd always been strong in mind, if not body, but all that would change when they got out of this mess. Stacey would have to learn self-defence so she could fight creeps later in life. They were like cockroaches, and they were everywhere.

She examined the crudely concreted room, the walls designed to block out light and sound. A perfect prison. Disgust filled her.

"This is what you call all right? What did you do to her?" she demanded as she stood, straightening her spine and joining him at his level, staring him in the eye.

He appeared confused. "She wasn't you."

He'd answered her questions so simply, as if he wasn't talking about a human being. It sickened her.

"If you loved me, you wouldn't have done unspeakable acts to the person I love."

"She's nothing. Not you, Megan. Everything will be all right. We're together now."

"Just because you want me doesn't mean you can have me, you sick bastard." With Stacey safe, she no longer needed to continue the act. "What do you think was going to happen? That I'd be touched you wanted me, had gone to great lengths to take me, and that we'd live happily ever after? And they say women are dreamers."

Johnson flushed a deep red. "Shut up," he spat at her.

She didn't back down, placing her hands on her hips and glaring at him. "Why? The reality not living up to the dream, Johnson? You wanted me. Well, now you have me. Just as I am. This is me. This is what you wanted. Feeling foolish?" she taunted him.

A part of her knew she shouldn't taunt him. Despite his adoration, Johnson was still dangerous, but Megan couldn't seem to back away. Not even when his hands became fists by his sides, the vein in his temple throbbing a fast tempo. What he'd done to Stacey was unforgiveable.

"Stop it. You shouldn't—"

"What, have a brain? You're thinking of a blow up doll, Johnson."

He moved in close to her, close enough she could smell his rancid breath and his body odour mixed with his spicy cologne. His large hands grabbed hold of her shoulders, pushing at her roughly, and she struggled against him, kicking at

290

him, her foot connecting with his shin. He caught hold of her left arm and jerked it around her back in an effort to control and limit her movements, the force of the unnatural angle dislocating her shoulder and she screamed out in agony. White-hot pain like she'd never before experienced shot up and down her arm, spreading throughout her body.

***

Dean hit the brakes hard, coming to an abrupt stop outside Johnson's house south of the city limits where neighbours were few and far between. The sudden decline of speed jerked him in his seat and he knew he'd have a bruise across his chest from the seat belt in the morning. He climbed out of his car and before his feet even touched the ground another three vehicles stopped, the first just centimetres from his own.

He glanced at the house. Megan was somewhere inside there. He was going to get her back and then he'd never let her go. He was scared and didn't deny it. Emma's bloody body popped inside his mind before he ruthlessly pushed it away. Megan wasn't Emma and he wasn't going to lose her. History would not repeat itself.

For years he'd been too fearful of letting anyone get close to him, knowing if he cared even just a little bit he would be weak and vulnerable, but Megan had slipped past all his defences and he was grateful. He loved her and he planned on telling her the very first chance he got. He wanted a future and he wanted it with Megan.

Failure was not an option.

He gave Matt a nod, one that told him of his gratitude before making his way up the walkway towards the house. He was almost at the door when he heard a woman scream, followed by two words he'd never forget for as long as he lived.

"Megan, no!"

Dean's heart lodged in the vicinity of his throat, his hand automatically going for his gun, withdrawing it from the tan leather holster. The heavy feeling of it was natural in his hand as he kicked opened the front door with one well-placed hit.

Chapter 45

Megan didn't allow him any more opportunities to subdue her, stamping down hard on his instep, startling him as she pulled her good arm back and sent a fist into his sternum, winding him. She ignored her throbbing shoulder. It would only bring her down. She fought against the searing pain and the darkness threatening to consume her. She knew he had more strength then her, but he also wasn't prepared for her attack and she used that against him.

Johnson barely had time to double over in agony before she moved her body onto an angle, swinging her arm towards his face, gaining momentum. Her fist connected with his nose and she heard the satisfying crunch as the delicate bones broke, blood spurted out and began to form a river down his chin. She raised her knee sending it flying into his family jewels as she poked at his eyes with her fingers, meeting the squishy grape-like corneas.

The room filled with his cries as she backed away from him, breathing heavily from the exertion. He fell to the floor, his hands moving over his body, unsure of which hurt body part to hold first. Megan's gaze searched the makeshift prison for a weapon but she needn't have bothered. In a matter of seconds, the door flung open and Dean, looking his most fierce, gun raised, finger resting against the trigger, scanned the room for danger. He glanced briefly at the incapacitated man on the floor for a second before moving on. His gaze met hers and she visibly saw his body relax.

"Meg," was all he said, but she heard so much more in his voice.

She smiled, her vision blurred. A lone tear escaped to roll down her cheek. She liked to believe it was brought about from the sight of Dean more than the searing pain.

"Dean."

He strode towards her with intention. She launched herself across the small distance and into his arms, the nightmare that was Johnson all but forgotten. Dean held her close as if he had no intention of letting her go any time soon, her feet dangling in the air.

Out of the corner of her eye she saw Dean's team cuff Johnson none too gently and knew that everything was going to be all right. How could it not when she was in the arms of Dean Matthews?

Megan wrapped her uninjured arm around his neck, letting the left dangle beside her thigh and held onto him tightly. She kissed him with everything she had, deeply and completely. She had known he would come, that Dean would find her. She'd been scared, though, completely out of her element. Now she was thankful she had gone through that, knowing that when the chips were down she could hold her own. Life was unreliable and moments like these were precious. Whatever would happen in the future, she wasn't about to mess it up by believing she had all the time in the world.

"I'm sorry," he said the moment his lips left hers. "I was afraid. You touched a place inside me no one ever has. I lashed out, hurting the one person I never wanted to harm. I wish we could go back and change the past. I can't erase my words or actions but I promise to try to make it up to you. For however long it takes. If you'll let me."

The words she'd longed to say tumbled out of her mouth. "I love you."

As her heart hammered, her lungs constricted, stealing her breath as she waited to see how he'd take the news. She knew he had issues when it came to relationships and emotions, and she didn't want to scare him off, but she couldn't go another second without telling him what was in her heart.

Dean took her face in his hands and stared deeply into her eyes. His own were so full of emotion that she trembled.

"I love you too, Meg. Don't ever leave me."

Her breath left in a rush as her heart filled with joy. "Not a chance," she promised with a smile.

Nick glided past them, a limping and handcuffed Kenneth Johnson being pushed in front of him. He shot her a menacing look through his already blackening eyes. She glared right back. She would not cower before him. Not now. Not ever.

295

Dean took possession of her mouth again, clearing her mind of everything but him. She loved the taste of him and savoured it as his tongue tangled with her own, robbing her of breath.

Nick shook his head and muttered, "Get a room."

"My thoughts exactly," Stacey added as she slowly moved towards them, assisted by James. Her body swayed slightly under the force it took to stay on her feet. Her arms wrapped around her small waist. "Megan, honey, are you going to stop sticking your tongue down his throat long enough to introduce us?"

Epilogue

Megan stepped into the hospital room, her arm held tight against her body in a sling while her shoulder recovered, Dean a step behind her. He nodded to his team and their wives who all stood surrounding Kellie's bed, her newborn son cuddled in her arms. Her head rested on Darryl's shoulder and his arm was wrapped tightly around her. She appeared exhausted but happy and smiled as they approached.

Megan handed Nick the bouquet of flowers she'd been holding in her good hand and he added them to the already large collection covering every available surface.

"Congratulations." She leaned over Darryl to get a look at the newest Hill. "He is so cute."

"He takes after his mother," Darryl told her and kissed Kellie's head tenderly.

Megan smiled. Little Cameron Hill really was the cutest thing she'd ever seen. His tiny fist was curled against his mother's chest and his little pink lips made a sucking motion. A hand pressed against

297

her back as Dean joined her.

"Thank goodness," he said, shaking Darryl's hand.

Kellie rolled her eyes. "Wanna hold him?" She shifted and held Cam up towards Dean. His eyes momentarily lit up with panic before it was banked and he took the offered baby, securing him in his strong arms.

Megan's heart melted as Dean settled the baby against his chest. He was so tiny and delicate in the big hands of his 'uncle,' but continued to sleep soundly. Her stomach flipped, an aching tenderness swallowing her up. Dean looked so ferocious all the time, she'd never expected him to be gentle and caring when it came to children—first Maddie and now Cam.

She retrieved her phone from her pocket and Dean's chin lifted as she took a photo of them and he winked at her. She reached over and stroked the palm of Cam's hand with her thumb and she swore her heart skipped a beat.

"Are you going to give me one of these?" Dean asked her quietly, low enough that she was the only one to hear him.

She gave him a long look as she determined how serious he was. He stared back at her, unflinching. She smiled at him and whispered in his ear, "How soon can we leave?"

Acknowledgements

As always, there are a fabulous troop of people I'd like to thank. My editor, Rosa for making all my books special. Also, the wonderful, talented team at Limitless Publishing who've helped me realise my dream to hold my book in my hands. Another heartfelt thanks goes out to my fellow authors, who are the most supportive friends a girl could ask for, you're all awesome! To the bloggers and my fantastic new street team, Camille's Cohorts, I'm forever grateful for your hard work spreading the word. And lastly, my readers: thank you for letting me share my world with you.

About the Author

Camille Taylor is an Australian author who resides in the Nation's Capital with her small dog. She was the typical 90's kid and was raised on Goosebumps, Roald Dahl and Paul Jennings. In her teens she began reading the Queen of Crime, Agatha Christie and in later years found Christine Feehan, Janet Evanovich and Julie Garwood.

She started writing at sixteen and enjoys spending time with her family, doting on her nieces and nephews, writing the many stories floating about her head and working on her genealogy where she can trace her heritage to England, Scotland, Ireland and Russia.

Her other interests include, anything creative— such as scrapbooking and drawing and has travelled across Western Europe, New Zealand and the UAE, after spending a year living in London. She's also dabbled in tae kwon do.

Facebook:
https://www.facebook.com/CamilleTaylorAuthor

Twitter:
https://twitter.com/CamilleTaylorAu

Website:
https://camilletaylorbooks.wordpress.com/

Goodreads:
https://www.goodreads.com/author/show/7791241.
Camille_Taylor

Newsletter:
http://eepurl.com/bxuOar